# Finding Hope

# Finding Hope

# NICOLA BAKER

Illustrated by Rachael Dean

SIMON & SCHUSTER

First published in Great Britain in 2024 by Simon & Schuster UK Ltd

Celebrating 100 Years of Publishing in 2024

1 3 5 7 9 10 8 6 4 2

Simon & Schuster UK Ltd
1st Floor, 222 Gray's Inn Road
London WC1X 8HB

www.simonandschuster.co.uk
www.simonandschuster.com.au
www.simonandschuster.co.in

Simon & Schuster Australia, Sydney
Simon & Schuster India, New Delhi

A CIP catalogue record for this book is available
from the British Library.

HB ISBN 978-1-3985-2716-4
eBook ISBN 978-1-3985-2718-8
eAudio ISBN 978-1-3985-2717-1

Printed and Bound in the UK using
100% Renewable Electricity at CPI Group (UK) Ltd

MIX
Paper | Supporting
responsible forestry
FSC® C171272

For Matthew, Luke and Molly

# Chapter One

# ABANDONED

Ava squeezed her mum tight, fighting against the lump in her throat.

'We'll be back before you know it, love,' said her dad.

Ava's mum kissed her lightly on the forehead, brushing Ava's dark brown hair away from her face. 'Don't worry – it's only for a couple of weeks. There'll be plenty to keep you busy on the farm with Aunt Kitty and Uncle John. It'll be fun,' she said softly.

Ava nodded, forcing a smile as she looked at her mum.

'I'm just going to miss you both, that's all.'

Ava's mum pulled her into a tight hug, which Ava wished would never end.

'We've left you a little something in your room. You can open it when we've gone,' Ava's mum whispered in her ear.

'Time to go. We don't want to miss our flight!' said Ava's dad.

Ava reluctantly stepped back and watched her parents climb into the car. She watched the car drive away along the farm track and caught sight of her mum waving enthusiastically at her. Ava waved back, her heart heavy as they rounded the corner and out of sight. She blinked back tears. She'd promised herself she wouldn't cry, and a promise was a promise, even if it was to yourself.

The green fields, hedgerows and woodland came

into sharp focus around her in the early morning sunlight. Ava glanced over her shoulder at her aunt and uncle's farmhouse. Its grey stone walls and white windows with their colourfully planted window boxes always made her feel welcome. But she didn't feel like going inside just yet.

Ava hoisted herself up onto a wooden fence and breathed in a deep lungful of countryside air. It felt clean and fresh, not at all like the air back at home in the city. The sounds around her were different too – the wind gently rustling the trees, sheep bleating in the fields and the songs of countless birds – no traffic noise at all. This wasn't how she'd planned to spend her Easter holiday. Whistledown Farm was a long way from home and a world away from her usual life.

A puff of cherry blossom petals drifted in front of her, and she watched them float gracefully over the fence. Ava wrinkled her nose. She was sure her hay fever was kicking in.

3

'All right, sweetheart?'

Ava looked up to see her aunt standing nearby. She gave her a small smile, hoping it would reassure Aunt Kitty.

'I've made hot chocolate and those ginger biscuits you like. I know you love them when they're warm,' said Aunt Kitty brightly.

Ava sighed. This was it for the next couple of weeks – farm life and no Mum and Dad. Maybe a warm ginger biscuit would make it hurt a little less?

The welcoming smell of ginger wafted towards Ava as she stepped into the farmhouse kitchen. Her cousin Tom was already helping himself to the stack of biscuits. Ava sat down at the worn wooden table as Tom reached for another one.

'You might want to change out of those nice clothes,' he mumbled, with his mouth full. 'There's loads to do today, so you can't just sit around.'

Ava's Aunt Kitty put a mug of hot chocolate on the table with a bang, making Tom jump. Ava tried to hide her smile when she saw Aunt Kitty's unimpressed face.

'What?' asked Tom. 'She can't wander around like she's on holiday as she normally does when she comes to visit. She's here for a couple of weeks, and we're really busy now it's lambing time. Dad said she had to help!'

'She will, Tom. Won't you, love?' Aunt Kitty looked at Ava.

Ava slowly swallowed her biscuit as she felt the weight of her aunt's expectant stare. Ava wasn't really an animal person, or even an outdoor person, and neither were her parents. In fact, Ava could hardly believe her mum and Aunt Kitty were sisters at all, they were such opposites. It wasn't that Ava didn't *like* animals; they'd just never been part of her life before – she wasn't allowed any pets at home because her parents were too busy with work. When her family visited Whistledown Farm, they didn't get involved in any of the 'animal duties'. If she was supposed to muck in now, she wouldn't know what to do and doubted she'd be any good at it anyway.

'See, she doesn't want to help!' said Tom, reaching for another biscuit.

'Tom will show you the ropes, don't worry, love,' said Aunt Kitty, directing a warm smile at Ava.

Ava narrowed her dark brown eyes at her cousin. She didn't dislike Tom; it was more that they had absolutely nothing in common. Tom spent every possible moment outside doing farm work, and Ava always got the impression that he didn't want her in the way. They never seemed to have much to talk about either.

'That's settled then,' said Aunt Kitty, whipping

6

away the half-eaten biscuits. 'Time waits for nobody, especially when you have a farm to run. Ava, why don't you get yourself settled in first. You can meet Tom outside when you've unpacked.'

Ava nodded unenthusiastically and made her way upstairs, sidestepping the sleeping black-and-white cat on the top step. Ava's room was at the far end of the landing – the one she normally shared with her parents. She opened the door with a soft squeak and sighed as she looked around. It was just her this time. Ava's suitcase was by the wardrobe and the size of it made her stomach ache – it was much bigger than the overnight bag she usually brought.

Ava couldn't face unpacking, so instead she flopped onto the bed. Something on the bedside table caught her eye, shimmering in the morning sunshine that seeped in through the window. It was a neatly wrapped package with a large silver bow.

The corner of Ava's mouth twitched into a smile –
her mum had said they'd left something for her! She
tore off the paper to reveal a small box.

'A phone . . .' she breathed.

Ava had never been allowed a phone before.
She eagerly opened the lid to check that there was
*actually* one inside – her dad liked to play practical
jokes and she really hoped this wasn't one of them.
A folded piece of paper slipped out and Ava caught
the smell of her mum's perfume as she opened the
note. It smelt like home.

*We can't wait to hear about your farm adventures!*
*Ring any time. We love you,*
*Mum and Dad xx*

The bedroom door creaked open and Aunt Kitty's head popped round. She'd tied her light brown hair back with a blue headscarf that matched the colour of her eyes.

'I just came to see if you needed any help,' said Aunt Kitty, coming to sit beside her. Aunt Kitty's eyes fell on the phone in Ava's lap. 'You opened it then?'

Ava nodded, staring at the phone.

'We'll get it set up and you can ring your mum and dad whenever you want,' said Aunt Kitty softly.

A tear slid down Ava's cheek as she felt Aunt Kitty's arm round her shoulders.

'We'll have fun, I promise!' said her aunt brightly. 'Besides, my job lists are legendary in this family.

I'll make yours so long, you'll be too busy to notice they're gone – two weeks will fly by!'

Ava looked at her aunt, eyes wide in shock. Aunt Kitty started laughing and Ava realized with relief that her aunt was only joking.

'Time will go faster if you get stuck in though,' said Aunt Kitty, giving Ava a squeeze. 'Try to make the most of it here, sweetheart. You never know, you might even enjoy yourself.'

## Chapter Two

# FRESH EGGS
# AND FARM WORK

An hour later, Ava found Tom waiting outside. As soon as he saw her, he strode away towards the farmyard, his light brown hair ruffling in the breeze.

'Wait up,' called Ava, trying to jog in her brand-new green wellies. She winced as they pinched at her feet.

Tom didn't slow down until he reached the door of the chicken barn and turned to face Ava.

'Just do what I say, okay?' said Tom bossily.

'Fine,' said Ava, resisting the urge to answer back.

They may have both been ten, but Tom was a few months older and didn't let Ava forget it. He was also a few centimetres taller, but Ava was definitely catching up.

Tom headed inside and Ava made sure to stay right on his heels.

'Feed, shavings and straw are in there.' Tom pointed to the left.

Ava peered into the small storeroom, noting the items.

'Use the shovel, broom and wheelbarrow to clean out the chicken pens, and empty the wheelbarrow when you're done.'

Ava nodded.

'Most of the chickens are out in the field, so now's a good time to muck out their pens. There'll be the odd chicken wandering back in to lay, but that'll be it.'

'Eggs?' said Ava, feeling a prickle of excitement.

'No . . . chocolate bars!' said Tom, rolling his eyes. 'Course they're laying eggs, Ava.'

Ava smiled, despite her cousin's sarcasm. 'I haven't *actually* seen a chicken lay an egg. That's so cool.'

She realized Tom was momentarily taken aback by her enthusiasm. He must have seen so many freshly laid eggs on the farm.

'Well, if you have a look before you muck out, you'll probably find some from this morning,' said Tom with a shrug.

Ava smiled and let herself into the first chicken pen.

'They'll be at the back in the nest boxes,' said Tom. 'I'll start filling the feeders.'

Ava made her way to the boxes filled with straw. As she got closer, she could see that there were a dozen or so eggs dotted around – brown, white and blue ones too. A huge grin crept across her face as she began to pick them up, trying hard not to break any but struggling to hold them all.

'Here,' said Tom, handing her a basket.

Ava carefully placed the eggs inside.

'This one's warm!' she cried, holding it out to Tom.

Tom laughed. 'Course it is – it's just come out of a chicken!'

'But it's *really* warm!'

'I guess so.' Tom shrugged with a small smile. 'There's nothing better than a fresh egg for breakfast, if you ask me.'

Ava's face fell. 'Are there chicks inside? Will these eggs hatch?'

'No, there's no cockerel in with these hens, so the eggs won't get fertilized and become chicks.' Tom pointed to the next pen. 'The eggs in there are from Dad's show chickens and the ones we sell. They should hatch.'

'Is that one laying an egg right now?' Ava pointed to a lone white chicken in the neighbouring pen.

Tom shook his head. 'No, she's sitting.'

'She's what?' asked Ava.

'She's been sitting on a batch of eggs for a couple of weeks, so there should be chicks hatching soon.'

'Really!' cried Ava, her eyes wide with excitement.

'I thought you weren't an animal person?' said Tom.

Ava shrugged. 'Baby chicks are pretty cute!'

Tom's green eyes squinted at her in confusion.

'Anyway, we'd better crack on or we'll never get finished,' he said.

Ava put the last of the morning's eggs into the basket and looked down at the wood shavings covering the floor. She wrinkled her nose at the dollops of chicken poo scattered around, wishing in that very moment she was playing in the park at home instead.

Ava realized that Tom had stopped what he was doing to look at her. She grabbed the shovel and set to work – she wasn't going to give Tom an excuse to complain that she wasn't doing her farm jobs. Ava began to heap the dirty bedding into the wheelbarrow, trying not to let her face show she thought it was a bit smelly in the barn. She glanced over at Tom, who had started to fill the chicken drinkers with water. He moved with such a quick confidence that Ava was sure he could do these jobs blindfolded. Ava was determined to prove that she could be useful, so she watched Tom carefully, taking note of what he was doing so she could try and impress him by doing the same tomorrow.

The door to the barn opened and Uncle John appeared in the doorway. He looked just as he always did – blue overalls covered his strong, tall frame, topped off with a cap and black wellies. Ava had never seen him look any different.

'Morning, Ava. Welcome back to Whistledown Farm! Nice to see you're getting stuck in already.' Uncle John's smile widened. 'There's a lamb on its way if you fancy helping out?'

Ava's heart began pounding. 'A lamb?' she asked tentatively.

'Yes, Ava. We're a sheep farm – we do have a few!' Her uncle's green eyes twinkled with amusement.

Ava hadn't expected to feel the excitement that was

fizzing inside her – she'd never seen *anything* being born before. Today was definitely a day of firsts!

'Do you need me too, Dad?' asked Tom, looking up from his work.

'I'll just take Ava. It should be quite simple, but I'll shout if I need another pair of hands.'

Ava put down her shovel and followed her uncle.

'Oh, Ava,' shouted Tom, as she reached the door, 'the dirty bedding will still be here when you're done with Dad.'

# Chapter Three

# THE LAMBING SHED

Ava walked with Uncle John towards the lambing shed. The late morning sun peeked out from behind the clouds, its gentle spring warmth welcome on Ava's face.

'You okay?' asked her uncle. His usual matter-of-fact tone had been replaced with a softer one, catching Ava off guard.

'Yeah, fine,' replied Ava, avoiding his gaze. She knew why he was asking.

'Your parents will be back before you know it,' he said gently.

Ava sighed.

'I know. I just wish I could have gone with them.'

Uncle John put his arm round her shoulders.

'They did want you to, but they're going to be so tied up with work while they're over in America – they just thought you'd be bored and lonely.'

Ava knew her uncle was right. It wouldn't have been much fun if she'd gone with her parents; they were always busy, even when they were at home. They were both medical research scientists and loved their work. They'd met on their very first job and worked together ever since. They were on their way to Chicago to start trials on a new antibiotic they'd been working on for the last few years. Ava knew their work was really important, but that didn't mean she wasn't going to miss them – *and* they'd never been this far away before.

'What if they like it over there, Uncle John? What if they get offered a permanent job and don't come back?' asked Ava anxiously.

'Of course they'll come back! Try not to worry, Ava. Although, it could be fun to live in America, don't you think?'

Ava didn't know what to say. She liked her life at home well enough, but school hadn't been the same since her best friend, Talia, had moved away last year. They'd barely spoken since and she really missed her. To fill her spare time, and encouraged by her parents to find something she loved, she'd spent ages trying to work out what she liked to do. Ava knew they were passionate about science and saving the world – but the hours of art classes, swimming, archery, STEM courses and everything else she tried still hadn't sparked excitement in her. Ava hadn't made any new friends either as she never stuck at anything for long.

A wave of loneliness washed over her. Honestly, she thought it wouldn't matter if she did move halfway round the world; there was nothing to really keep her here. Ava realized her uncle was looking at her, waiting for her to say something. She gave him a shrug – he probably wouldn't understand how she felt.

'Welcome to the lambing shed!' said Uncle John brightly, stopping in front of a large wooden building. 'I can't believe you've never been in here.'

He was right – she'd never ventured down to the lambing shed. In fact, she'd never explored the farm much at all. She had to admit though, so far she was actually enjoying herself today. Ava suddenly felt bad that she hadn't made more of an effort before.

Ava followed her uncle into the enormous shed. It was warm, protected from the wind outside, and there was a cosy layer of straw on the floor. About thirty sheep were enclosed in a large area at the

back, with a few single sheep and their newborn lambs in individual pens along the side.

'These are our *high-maintenance* sheep, as your Aunt Kitty likes to call them,' said Uncle John with a smile. 'There's a mix of our pedigree sheep we take to the shows, as well as a handful of hill sheep that've had problems giving birth in the past.'

'There are more sheep than this?' asked Ava, staring at the abundance of animals around her.

'Loads more!' said Uncle John with a grin. 'The rest are happier to give birth out on the hills. They'll wander off somewhere quiet and come back a few hours later with a lamb or two in tow.'

'But don't they need help?'

Uncle John smiled at her. 'Nature is a wonderful thing, Ava. They're well prepared for life out there, and most sheep are really good mums.'

A strange grunting noise from the back of the shed caught Ava's attention.

'Ah, that's her.' Uncle John pointed towards a large white sheep in the corner.

'Is she okay?' asked Ava. The sheep grunted again and Ava watched it begin to pant.

'She's in the full swing of labour,' said Uncle John. 'Won't be long now. Look, she's pushing hard.'

The sheep's head tilted upwards as its whole body contracted.

'Can we help her?' whispered Ava with a hint of worry.

'No need. She's doing fine by herself.'

Ava was transfixed as the sheep panted and pushed. Her emotions were swirling inside her – she was excited to see the new lamb, worried something would go wrong and a little grossed out by what was about to happen, all at the same time.

The sheep shifted its position and threw her head back again. With one mighty push, it stood up, and Ava could see something dark and wet lying on the straw. She craned her neck to get a better look – the dark shape wasn't moving.

Ava felt a bubble of panic. 'Uncle John . . .' she whispered.

'Give her a minute,' he said calmly.

'Uncle John . . .' said Ava more urgently.

The sheep began to lick the lamb. Ava watched her remove the gooey substance around the lamb's face. The sheep bleated gently at its lamb, continuing to lick and nudge. It bleated again and again . . . until suddenly the lamb sneezed in reply.

Ava gasped. She remained transfixed, eyes wide as the tiny newborn lifted its head and bleated at its mother.

Uncle John nudged Ava.

'She's a first-time mum – she just needed a moment to realize what was happening.'

Ava's eyes prickled with tears; she couldn't believe she'd just seen new life come into the world.

'Amazing, isn't it?' said her uncle softly. 'Gets me every time. Like I said, nature is a wonderful thing.'

Ava couldn't tear her eyes away from the newborn lamb. The mother had begun to nudge it again, encouraging it to stand. The lamb bleated softly and pushed up on its front legs before collapsing.

'Keep watching,' said Uncle John.

The lamb pushed up again, this time managing to stand for a brief moment before falling down. With another gentle nudge from its mother, the lamb heaved itself up again, wobbling but upright, on its tiny, unsteady legs.

Ava gasped. 'I can't believe it's standing already!'

Her uncle laughed. 'Yep. It took you a year to do that!'

Ava smiled at her uncle and felt her heart swell with happiness. The lamb began nuzzling underneath its mother, searching for a drink.

'You know it's drinking properly when its tail

shakes happily like that,' pointed out Uncle John. 'This little one is going to be just fine.'

A huge grin spread across Ava's face. 'I could watch this for ever.'

# Chapter Four

# THE RESCUE

At lunchtime, Aunt Kitty brought cheese and pickle sandwiches to the lambing shed, with glasses of lemonade to wash them down. Ava munched hungrily as her uncle told her about the different breeds of sheep on the farm and all about taking the pedigree ones to the county shows. There was so much she didn't know, and she felt a bit guilty that she'd never spent this much time with her uncle before.

Ava spent the rest of the afternoon watching

intently for signs that another sheep might give birth. Much to her disappointment, there had been nothing, but her uncle had said most lambs were born first thing in the morning or at dusk.

'I thought you were coming back to finish your jobs.'

Tom was standing in the doorway and he didn't look happy.

Ava started to explain. 'There was a sheep that gave birth and . . .'

'Ewe. The female sheep are called ewes, Ava. Everyone knows that,' snapped Tom.

'Now, now, Tom,' said Uncle John, shooting him a warning look.

Ava didn't let Tom dampen her excitement. 'It was wonderful, Tom! I can't wait to see another lamb being born.'

Tom folded his arms across his chest and glared at Ava.

'Anyway, I've finished everything *you* were supposed to do.'

'Oh . . . I'm sorry, Tom – I did mean to come back. I just got caught up in here.' Ava hoped Tom would understand.

'I came to let Dad know I'll check on the hill sheep now.'

'I can do that!' offered Ava.

'You don't have to,' said Uncle John.

'No, honestly, I want to.'

'It's quite a walk up to the top fields, Ava,' her uncle replied.

'That's fine,' said Ava. 'It'll give me time to explore.'

'Try not to get lost,' sniped Tom as he stomped away.

Ava's face fell.

Uncle John smiled apologetically at Ava. 'I'll have a word with him later.'

'It's okay. I didn't go back to finish my jobs.

I wouldn't be happy if I was Tom. Please let me go and check on the sheep – I just want to help.'

Her uncle hesitated, then nodded. 'Okay. It would save us a job, and there's nothing to it really. Do you know where you're going?'

'Sort of.'

'Just head up to the hill fields at the side of the farmhouse. Do a loop around to make sure everything looks okay so we can head in for the evening knowing the hill flock are fine. No sheep are limping, stuck in fences, that sort of thing. If something doesn't seem right, anything at all, come and let me know. Then we can go and sort it together.'

'Okay,' said Ava, trying to sound more confident than she felt.

'It's not often there's anything amiss, so it should just be a nice late afternoon walk,' said Uncle John with a smile.

Ava trudged along the fence-line of the hill field that bordered the woodland. Everything had been quiet so far, but as she glanced up at the next field, she was beginning to regret volunteering. The hill was steep and she was already getting tired traipsing through the thick, tufty grass. Ava gritted her teeth at the pain from her new wellies as they rubbed her ankles. In hindsight, trainer socks were probably not the best choice. But she was determined not to give up – she wanted to prove she could be helpful.

At the corner of the next field, something colourful caught her eye on the other side of the fence. She bent down for a closer look. It was a pile of discarded crisp packets, chocolate wrappers and a plastic bottle. Ava tried to reach through the wire fence to pick them up, but it was too far. She couldn't imagine anyone at Whistledown Farm would drop litter, so who had left it there? She resolved to come back and pick it up, but for now she had to finish her checks.

Ava continued on and her mind drifted to her parents. Were they nearly in Chicago? Did they miss her? She really missed them. Ava hoped they'd call soon. She ignored the knot of sadness in her stomach, scanning the field to distract herself. The black sheep around her all seemed happy enough, only giving her a quick glance before continuing to munch on the grass. Some had lambs close by, while others must still be waiting for theirs to arrive.

Ava stopped still for a moment at the very top of the hill, looking back down the way she'd come. The gentle spring breeze felt wonderfully cool on her skin. There was nothing but sheep, grass and trees for miles around, with only the odd farm dotted here and there across the valley. The local village was a ten-minute drive away and the nearest town almost an hour. This seemed impossible to Ava, who had three corner shops within five minutes' walk of her house. She could walk to school too, but knew Tom had to be driven to his. Ava wondered if Tom had lots of friends there.

Since Talia had moved away, Ava hadn't made any new friends at school, so it wasn't as much fun as it used to be. She pushed away her unwelcome thoughts and sank to the grass for a moment to catch her breath. She couldn't see the farmhouse from here, and with the fields stretching out around her, she felt totally alone.

The setting sun disappeared behind a thick band of grey cloud. It was beginning to get dark, and rain was threatening. Ava stood up to head back in the general direction of the farmhouse. As she passed a large clump of yellow gorse, she felt the first drop of rain on her face. She quickened her pace, then stopped – she thought she'd heard something strange.

Ava listened carefully. The only things she could catch were the breeze and distant bleats of the sheep behind her. She stood still, a light patter of rain settling on her cheeks. But there it was again. A soft squeaking sound coming from the gorse. Ava knelt down and peered into the dark undergrowth. A flicker of movement caught her eye and Ava's heart raced.

'H-hello?' said Ava, her voice cracking.

Something rustled.

'Hello?'

*Baa.*

Ava jumped at the sound.

*Baa.*

It was soft and feeble, but it sounded like a lamb.

'Come on out, little one,' encouraged Ava, catching a glimpse of a tiny dark shape.

It didn't move, so Ava stayed as still as she could, hoping she wouldn't frighten it.

The lamb lurched clumsily towards her.

'That's it. Come on out,' said Ava softly.

A tiny black lamb stumbled out from under the gorse, and Ava backed away, giving it space. It wobbled unsteadily before collapsing.

'Ooops,' said Ava, diving forward to set the lamb back on its feet.

Ava and the lamb looked at each other.

*Baaa.*

'Where's your mum?' whispered Ava.

She stood up and scanned the field. Ava didn't know much about sheep yet, but she remembered her uncle mentioning that mothers made a lot of noise when they were separated from their lambs – and she couldn't hear any frantic bleating. The lamb took a few unsteady steps towards her.

*Baa.*

Ava glanced at the farmhouse in the distance. It was a long walk back – what was she *supposed* to do? Ava stared at the lamb shivering in the rain. One thing she did know was that it shouldn't be on its own.

'Stay there while I find your mum,' said Ava, moving away.

*Baaaaaaaaa.*

The lamb's bleat was louder now, more insistent. Ava hesitated.

'Do you want to come with me? Shall we find your mum together?'

Ava gathered the lamb in her arms. Its black fleece was a little sticky against her skin, and she could feel its tiny ribs expanding with each breath. She held it gently, unsure if she was holding it right. Ava made her way back up the hill towards the main flock of sheep. As she got closer, the sheep began to move away from her.

'How can I find your mum in this lot?' she muttered to the lamb.

The lamb bleated loudly. A couple of the sheep turned to look at them.

'That's it – keep going,' urged Ava.

The lamb fell silent.

'Okay. Here goes nothing,' said Ava, taking a deep breath. '*Baa.*'

A few of the sheep looked up.

'*Baa. Baa.*' Ava kept trying.

Most of the sheep were now staring at her. She gently placed the tiny lamb on the grass and backed away.

'Off you go, little one. Find your mum.'

Ava moved further back. The sheep nearest to her approached the lamb and sniffed it before ambling off. Ava turned away and headed down the hill, crossing her fingers. She hoped if she was further away and less of a distraction, it would give the lamb the best chance of reuniting with its mother. Glancing over her shoulder, she saw the lamb was standing alone, shouting mournfully – but none of the other sheep were calling back. Ava's stomach twisted.

'It's just a lamb,' she told herself. 'It'll find its mum. It'll be fine. Time to go, Ava.'

Ava walked towards the farmhouse, the lamb's

40

bleats ringing in her ears. She looked back, and her breath hitched in her throat – the lamb was trying to follow her! Ava picked up her pace. She risked another glance and was distraught to see the lamb still coming down the hill. That wasn't the plan – it was supposed to find its mum, not follow her! It stumbled and fell to the ground, and Ava froze, unsure what to do.

She couldn't leave it on its own – it was getting darker and colder. Her uncle had told her that newborn lambs were fine in the fields, but surely that wouldn't be the case for one that didn't have its mother?

*Baa.*

The lamb sounded quieter to Ava this time, weaker. She made her mind up and strode towards the lamb, picking it up. It was shivering – it felt much colder than it had before. She hurried down the hill, ignoring the chafing pain from her wellies and the rain drizzling against her face. The lamb felt limp in her arms and its ribs heaved with the effort of breathing. Ava pushed the lamb inside her jumper to keep it as warm as she could.

'Come on, little one. We need to get to the farmhouse. They'll know what to do with you.'

The lamb's breathing was ragged and erratic as she began to run towards the house.

'Stay with me,' Ava whispered to the tiny lamb. 'I'll look after you, I promise.'

# Chapter Five

# THE LAMB

Ava jogged into the farmyard, out of breath and clutching the lamb under her jumper. She skidded to a halt as she saw Tom emerge from the feed store. They locked eyes for a moment and Ava hesitated. She'd wanted to bump into Aunt Kitty or Uncle John first. Ava lowered her head and began to pace past her cousin, hoping he'd ignore her.

'Ava?'

She stopped and looked at Tom. He fixed his green eyes on her.

'What you up to?'

'Er, nothing,' she lied.

She realized she didn't sound very convincing at all. Tom's eyes travelled down to her bulbous jumper.

'What've you got there?'

Ava sighed.

'I was out on the hill and . . . and . . . I didn't know what to do. I had to save it, Tom.'

'Save what?' asked Tom with a furrowed brow.

Ava reluctantly pulled the lamb out from under her jumper. It gave a pitiful bleat.

'Ava!' shouted Tom. 'What have you done?'

Ava blinked in surprise.

'It was all alone. I couldn't leave it out there!'

Tom's cheeks reddened. 'You shouldn't have interfered!'

'I thought I was saving it!'

Tom opened his mouth to speak again but thought better of it. He stepped forward and grabbed Ava's sleeve, pulling her and the lamb out of the yard.

'Ow!' cried Ava.

As they emerged from the yard, Uncle John looked up from under the bonnet of his pick-up truck.

Tom shoved Ava in front of him.

'She didn't listen, Dad. She's brought a lamb down from the hill.'

Ava looked at her uncle as the shivering lamb bleated weakly. Tears had started running down her cheeks, and she turned away so Tom couldn't see.

'Why don't you head inside, Tom, and ask your mum to set up a box for the lamb. Tell her we'll be in soon,' said Uncle John, his face unreadable.

'But . . .' protested Tom.

'Go,' Uncle John said firmly.

Tom shook his head but did as he was told, leaving Ava and Uncle John in the drizzly early evening gloom.

'I don't understand what I've done wrong.'

'Just tell me what happened in the field, Ava,' said her uncle, putting his hands on his hips.

'I was checking the sheep, like you asked. I was on my way back when I heard this lamb,' said Ava, holding up the dark, quivering bundle. 'It'd been abandoned, Uncle John. I couldn't leave it there.'

'Where was it?' asked her uncle quietly.

'I found it under the gorse. It was all alone,' Ava sobbed.

Her uncle sighed but gave Ava a tight smile.

'It had probably been left there for safekeeping by its mum. That's why your cousin reacted like he did. He shouldn't have spoken to you like that though. Ava, I did tell you to come back and let me know if anything was wrong.'

'But it followed me. I couldn't leave it!'

Ava's tears were flowing fast and free. Her uncle gave her arm a gentle squeeze.

'Ava, love, I understand why you did what you did, but you should've left it in the gorse for us to check on later, after we'd given it every chance to reunite with its mother. If it was still alone in a little while, then we would have brought it in – but only as a last resort.'

'I'm sorry. I thought I was doing the right thing.' Ava wiped away a tear with the back of her hand.

'It's okay. It's done now,' said her uncle, giving Ava another squeeze. 'Let's get you both inside.'

They headed into the softly lit farmhouse. It was completely dark outside now, and Ava hadn't realized she was shivering almost as much as the tiny lamb. The warmth of the kitchen enveloped her like a welcome hug. She felt warmer still as she saw her aunt's reassuring smile as she stood in front of the old range oven with Tom.

'I'm sorry,' Ava mumbled, holding out the lamb.

Aunt Kitty took the lamb from Ava's trembling fingers.

'Oh my, little one. You're a skinny minny, aren't you? Chilly too. Apart from the bits you've warmed up though, Ava – good job.' Aunt Kitty gave Ava a wink.

Ava allowed herself a tiny smile as she watched her aunt place the lamb in a cardboard box, lined with a woollen blanket, in front of the oven.

'We'll get it warmed up properly, then try it with a drink,' said Aunt Kitty. Her brow creased for a moment. 'I don't like the sound of its breathing. It'll need antibiotics too.'

'I'll get them,' said Tom.

'It may not have been a bad thing that Ava decided to bring the poor thing back with her,' said Aunt Kitty, her face concerned.

Tom rolled his eyes. He grabbed the keys for the medicine cabinet and headed in the direction of the utility room.

Ava knelt down on the multicoloured rug beside her aunt and the box. The lamb bleated softly as Ava stroked its head.

'It's not been born long,' said her aunt.

'How do you know?' asked Ava.

'Look, you can still see the umbilical cord and it looks quite fresh. Can't be more than a few hours old.'

Tom returned with the medicine and handed it to his mum. Ava stroked the lamb gently. It didn't make a peep when Aunt Kitty gave it a shot of antibiotics. Ava could feel herself warming up as the minutes slowly ticked by, and she prayed the warmth of the kitchen was seeping into the lamb too.

After what felt like an eternity of anxious waiting,

Aunt Kitty finally seemed happier with the lamb's temperature, and Tom went to make up a bottle.

'Here,' said Tom, handing it to his mum.

Ava watched as Aunt Kitty gently pushed the rubbery teat of the bottle into the lamb's mouth, but most of the milk seemed to be seeping out of the corners.

'Why isn't it drinking?' asked Ava.

'It's just not used to it yet. We'll keep trying. It'll get the hang of it eventually.'

Ava continued to stroke the lamb, who had thankfully stopped shivering. Aunt Kitty held out the bottle to Ava.

'Why don't you have a go?'

'Me?' asked Ava, startled.

Aunt Kitty laughed gently.

'Yes, you, Ava!'

'But I don't know how to do it!'

'You won't know until you try,' said Aunt Kitty,

putting the bottle into Ava's hand.

Ava stared at the bottle and then at the lamb. Her stomach somersaulted. Why did she feel so nervous?

'Just give it a go,' said Aunt Kitty softly. 'I'll talk you through it.'

Ava tucked her long dark hair behind her ears and leaned forward. She pushed the teat towards the lamb's tiny mouth, while her aunt gently prised it open from the sides so Ava could slide it in.

'Now, hold it against the roof of its mouth so it chews on it a little.'

Ava watched the lamb, willing it to take a drink. After a few moments, the lamb began to chew.

'That's it, Ava. It'll soon realize there's something tasty in there and start drinking properly.'

Ava felt a gentle tug on the bottle and a smile began to creep across her tear-stained face.

'It's drinking, Aunt Kitty. It's drinking!'

Aunt Kitty smiled.

'I thought it might if you gave it the bottle, Ava – you're a natural.'

Ava beamed. The lamb continued to drink from the bottle, no longer chewing on it but taking great big satisfying gulps.

'It likes the milk,' said Ava, giving the lamb an encouraging stroke.

'It's not milk,' said Tom bluntly, still hovering in the kitchen. 'It's colostrum.'

Ava blinked at her cousin. 'But it looks like milk.'

'Any *proper* farmer knows that newborn lambs need colostrum. It's the first milk they drink from their mothers, which they can't get if they're carried off down hills. So I've had to make it a bottle with powdered stuff so it can get what it needs.'

'That's enough, Tom,' said Aunt Kitty firmly. 'Ava's still learning. Go and tell your dad tea's nearly ready.'

Tom rolled his eyes again and headed out of the kitchen.

'I really am sorry, Aunt Kitty. I didn't mean to do the wrong thing.'

'To be honest, Ava, if this one's mum didn't get back soon, we'd be doing this anyway. Besides, I hate to think what would've happened if you hadn't found it at all.'

'It will be okay though, won't it, Aunt Kitty?' asked Ava, her voice shaking.

Her aunt hesitated.

'I hope so, Ava.'

# KITCHEN CAMPSITE

The lamb managed to drink about a quarter of the colostrum milk. Ava was relieved to see its tummy now had a small bulge to it, and she felt a chink of pride that she'd been the one to get it to drink.

After a quick check from Uncle John, Ava now knew the newborn lamb was a girl. Ava was sat propped up against the warm oven, softly stroking the lamb in the box. It had slept through the delicious dinner Aunt Kitty had prepared for everyone. Meals at the farm always seemed to be made up of two courses, and Ava was beginning to like the promise of regular desserts. This evening's was sticky toffee pudding with custard – one of her all-time favourites.

Tom was standing at the sink, washing the dishes.

'Don't even think about giving her a name,' he said.

'Why not?' asked Ava. 'I've got to call her something.'

'No, you don't,' said Tom, rinsing the bubbles from a plate. 'Firstly, she might not make it. And secondly, if she does make it, she'll go back to the flock when she's ready. Either way, you'll get too attached, so it's pointless.'

Aunt Kitty had said the lamb wasn't out of the woods yet, but Ava silently wished she was through the worst.

'Honestly, Ava,' he said with a small sigh. 'Don't give it a name – not yet.'

Ava shrugged.

Tom finished the last of the dishes in silence before heading out of the kitchen, leaving Ava alone with the lamb.

'Please be okay,' she whispered. 'I promised you out on the hill that I'd look after you, and I will.'

The kitchen door opened, and Aunt Kitty bustled through, peeking at the sleeping lamb.

'She's toasty warm now,' said Ava with a grin.

'Her breathing still sounds rattly though,' said her aunt, who was preparing another bottle.

Ava watched her aunt mix the powdered colostrum formula with warm water.

'She will be okay though, won't she?' asked Ava.

'Hopefully, sweetheart, but sometimes they don't make it. Even when you think they're doing well.'

Ava felt a lump in her throat and her chest tightened. She couldn't bear the thought of breaking her promise to keep her safe. Aunt Kitty handed Ava the bottle and rubbed the lamb's black fleece to wake her. Ava eased the rubber teat into her mouth and she began to drink.

'You really do have the knack, Ava,' said her aunt.

Ava's cheeks flushed – she wasn't used to compliments. At school, she was average at just about everything, so didn't get that many. She hadn't found anything she was *really* good at yet either and was beginning to wonder if she ever would.

Ava watched as the lamb took more of the milk, until it finally pulled away from the bottle.

Ava beamed. 'She drank over half this time!'

The small black lamb rested her head on the woollen blanket, milk frothing at her mouth.

'Are you tired after that big drink?' asked Aunt Kitty softly. She ran her hand along the lamb's back a couple of times before resting it on her chest. Ava realized she was feeling the lamb breathe. The tiniest lines of concern creased Aunt Kitty's forehead, making Ava's stomach twist.

'Can I stay with her tonight?' Ava blurted out.

Aunt Kitty looked as though she was trying to make up her mind.

'I don't see why not. I can make you up a little bed next to the box. You can keep an eye on her.'

Ava flung her arms round her aunt, breathing in the scent of outdoors and baking, which always made her feel warm and welcome.

'Thank you!'

'It's probably the only chance you'll get any sleep tonight anyway!' Aunt Kitty said with a laugh. 'Besides, it means I won't need to get up as often, if you're going to feed her.'

Ava stared wide-eyed at her aunt. 'What? On my own?'

'You'll be fine. I'll show you how to make the milk before I head to bed.'

A couple of hours later, Ava was tucked up in a sleeping bag next to the oven. Tom had gone up to bed muttering how ridiculous it was that she was sleeping with the lamb, and Uncle John had raised an eyebrow but said nothing. Aunt Kitty hovered by the kitchen door after she'd gone over how to make a bottle for the tenth time.

'I'm only upstairs if you need me.'

Ava nodded, not taking her eyes off the lamb, fast asleep in her box.

'Do ask for help if you need it, Ava. There are some things we can handle alone, but sometimes we all need to ask for help.'

'Okay, Aunt Kitty,' replied Ava. 'And I am sorry to have caused all this trouble.'

Aunt Kitty smiled.

'I think you made the right call. You may not have much experience with animals, but you listened to your gut.'

Ava felt her shoulders relax a little.

'I wish Tom felt the same,' she said with a sigh.

'He means well,' said Aunt Kitty. 'He's just not used to you wanting to be so involved in the farm. Once he understands you're here to help, he'll be fine.'

'I hope so, Aunt Kitty.'

'Your mum and dad would be so proud of you.'

Ava's chest tightened at the mention of her parents. She looked away to hide the tears that had started to well up.

'It's okay to miss them, Ava,' said Aunt Kitty softly.

Ava nodded.

'I'm sure they'll ring soon. They'll be back before

you know it too,' continued her aunt, her face full of concern. 'And until then, you've got this little one to look after, haven't you?'

Ava looked down at the sleeping lamb, a feeling of excitement rushing through her.

'You'll do a brilliant job. I know you will.'

'Thanks, Aunt Kitty,' replied Ava, the threat of tears subsiding.

'Oh, and don't tell Tom I told you this, but he slept in the chicken barn with the first set of chicks he hatched in the incubator.'

Ava's eyes widened in surprise.

'And he may not have slept in front of the oven, but he did stay in the lambing shed to keep watch over a lamb not unlike yours. You're not as different as you think,' said Aunt Kitty with a smile. 'Night, night, Ava.'

She switched off the main light, leaving Ava alone in the soft glow from above the oven. Warmth was still radiating from the range as Ava leaned against it. The heat sank deep into her body, warming her to her very bones. Suddenly she felt very tired. The exploits of her first day on Whistledown Farm were finally catching up with her. She had a feeling the next couple of weeks weren't going to be dull if today was anything to go by! She just hoped with all her heart that the lamb would be okay and perhaps the next few days would be a little less eventful. Ava snuggled down into her sleeping bag, suddenly knowing what she wanted to call the lamb.

'Goodnight, *Hope*,' she whispered. 'I'll look after you, I promise.'

# Chapter Seven

# CHICKENS . . .

At 7 a.m. the next morning, Tom burst into the kitchen, startling Ava, who was washing up the bottle from the lamb's morning feed. He peered into the cardboard box.

'Still alive then?'

'Of course she is,' said Aunt Kitty, coming in with a handful of fresh eggs.

Ava smiled. She could tell by Tom's face he'd been worried about the lamb but would never admit it.

'She took the whole bottle this morning,' Ava said proudly. 'And her breathing is getting better too.'

'Your cousin did a great job during the night, Tom – I hardly had to do a thing.'

'I've named her too,' said Ava, beaming. 'She's called Hope!'

Tom grunted and grabbed a slice of warm, buttery toast from the table. Ava sighed at his lack of enthusiasm for the name and her new-found farming skills.

'I've got to pop to the shops this morning as you two are eating me out of house and home!' said Aunt Kitty. 'Can I leave you both to get started outside? Your dad's down in the lambing shed already – he'll be there a good while by the sounds of it.'

Tom stopped eating and glanced across at Ava at the sink.

'Um. Okay. I'm sure we can get stuff started until you get back,' he said.

Ava tried to hide her smile, hoping Tom couldn't see how happy she was that he hadn't complained about having to work with her. She dried her hands on a tea towel and said goodbye to a soundly sleeping Hope.

'Come on, then,' said Tom, finishing the last of his toast.

Ava kept up with Tom as he veered towards the dog kennel in front of the house, a heavy-looking bowl in his hand. He crouched in front of the painted green kennel and placed the dog food on the ground. A sleepy black-and-white dog emerged and stretched out.

'Hello, boy,' said Tom, ruffling the dog's head.

Ava had completely forgotten about Tom's sheepdog. She had only stroked him once or twice on previous trips to the farm and realized

she couldn't even remember his name. She hadn't
met many dogs before, so felt a little nervous about
getting close to him. She'd just started to impress
Tom, and she wasn't going to stop now, so she
reached out to stroke him.

'No,' said Tom, stopping her hand in mid-air.
'Don't touch him when he's eating. He doesn't
know you very well and might think you're trying
to steal his breakfast. Ava, you need to be careful
around animals.'

'Oh. Sorry,' said Ava sheepishly.

'Think about it. How would you react if a stranger shoved their hand near your dessert? I saw how much you liked Mum's sticky toffee pudding last night!' He grinned. 'I reckon you'd try and protect that pudding at all costs.'

Ava laughed. He was probably right. She watched patiently as the dog finished his breakfast, licking the bowl clean.

'Good lad,' said Tom, crouching down to give him a hug.

Ava noticed how happy Tom was when he was with the animals. He seemed friendlier with her this morning too. Maybe he was getting used to her being around.

'Who's this, boy? Do you remember Ava?' asked Tom, ruffling the dog's coat.

Ava thought it very unlikely the dog would remember her.

'Okay, Ava, let Jet sniff your hand.'

Ava offered her hand to the Border collie. As Jet sniffed, Ava wondered if he could smell Hope too. Seemingly satisfied, Jet pushed his head under Ava's hand, letting her stroke him.

'He likes you,' said Tom with a surprised smile. 'Obviously doesn't know you well enough yet.'

He winked at Ava and flashed her a grin.

'Ha ha,' said Ava, giving Tom a gentle shove.

Ava laughed as Jet licked her neck.

'I could cuddle him all day!' she said.

'Maybe you could give him his tea later?' suggested Tom.

'I'd really like that, Tom. Thanks.'

Tom shrugged and stood up. 'Come on, then. As Dad says, "Time and tide wait for no one."'

Ava reluctantly prised herself away from Jet.

'What's next on the list?' she asked.

'We'll let the chickens out and feed up in the

69

barn, then check the water for the sheep in the front fields, and give the pony this –' Tom pulled a carrot from his pocket – 'if you promise not to tell Mum. He's supposed to be on a diet.'

Ava laughed. 'My lips are sealed.'

'We'll head down to the lambing shed after that and see if Dad needs any help. Then Mum will probably be back from the shops and have *another* massive list of jobs for us!'

The chicken barn was a symphony of sound.

'We're a little late this morning,' said Tom, letting himself into the first pen.

He opened a small door at the back that led out into the field where the chickens could roam freely. The noise level escalated as the chickens made a beeline for the grass beyond the door.

'Just like yesterday?' said Ava, picking up a feeder.

'Can you remember what to do?' asked Tom, raising an eyebrow in surprise.

'Think so,' replied Ava, trying to sound confident.

Tom went round to the next pen, opening it up to the outdoors. He stopped to pick up a small black-and-white chicken. Its feathers had the most beautiful pattern – Ava had never seen anything like it. They were a cross between fish scales and one of her nan's lace tablecloths. Tom held it close as he brought it over to Ava.

'This is HB,' he said, stroking the chicken's silky feathers. 'She's a Pencilled Wyandotte.'

Ava couldn't tear her eyes away from the hen.

'That's why I called her HB. You know, like the pencil.'

'Oh!' said Ava, realizing what he meant. 'That's clever!'

'HB's from a clutch of eggs I incubated a couple of years ago. She's really friendly. I've won a few

71

rosettes with her at the county show too.'

'Oh, nice,' said Ava, getting the impression she should be impressed.

'I often have long chats with HB. She's a good listener,' said Tom, giving Ava a smile.

Ava hesitated. She wasn't sure if Tom was joking.

'All I'm saying is, if you find yourself talking to the chickens, the rest of us do too. You won't be able to help yourself.'

'Okay . . .'

'Honestly, it's like they can actually talk back.'

Ava stroked HB, who was quiet and content in Tom's arms. *Chickens are funny-looking things*, she thought, *but quite lovely, nonetheless.*

It suddenly dawned on Ava that she hadn't even noticed the chicken *smell* today. Her mind drifted back to Hope, warm and snug in the kitchen . . . Maybe she was more of an animal person than she'd thought. She couldn't wait to tell her parents

about how she was getting stuck in on the farm –
they wouldn't believe it!

Tom put HB down, before nodding towards
a tiny brown cockerel. 'This little guy was my
first ever chicken. He's ancient now. Out you
go, Loki!' Tom gently shooed Loki towards the
open door. He fluffed out his chest feathers and
strutted away.

'Is Loki a pencil . . . thingy too?' asked Ava.

'Nah. He's a Serama. Smallest chickens in the
world! Mum and Dad let me look after him when
I was little. Their eggs are tiny, so don't make the
best breakfast, but Seramas have big personalities
and I like having them around the farm. Loki acts
like he owns the place!'

Ava marvelled at her cousin. His face lit up
whenever he talked about the animals, and this was
the longest conversation they'd ever had. Tom was
surprisingly chatty now that Ava had proved she

wasn't completely useless. She realized that she'd never asked him about any of this before. Ava had always expected Tom to make conversation with her. No wonder he thought she wasn't interested!

# Chapter Eight

# THE PHONE CALL

The next couple of days flashed by as Ava got used to the busy farm routine, trying to be as helpful as possible. She was feeling more confident around the animals, and Tom seemed to have mellowed and stopped complaining about having to work with her. He'd even trusted Ava to do some of the smaller tasks alone. She'd been allowed to keep sleeping in front of the oven with Hope too. The lamb was beginning to get stronger, and even Aunt Kitty thought she was out of danger.

Ava still hadn't managed to speak to her parents yet as the time difference meant they kept missing each other. Instead, she'd had to make do with text messages, which was better than nothing.

It was lunchtime, and Tom and Ava had finished their bigger jobs – the chickens were done, the sheep troughs checked, supplies replenished in the lambing shed, and Harris the Shetland pony had eagerly eaten his secret carrot.

Everyone sat round the farmhouse table while Uncle John filled them in on the latest news from across the valley – there was an upcoming farm sale and a couple of small thefts from farms in the next valley. He gave them all an update from the lambing shed too: there'd been three sets of early morning twins and a single lamb.

A loud bleating from in front of the oven interrupted Uncle John's update. Hope was standing up in her box.

'You're doing a grand job with that lamb, Ava,' said Uncle John. 'Nearly time for her to move out.'

'Out where?' asked Ava, panic edging her voice.

Uncle John laughed.

'Well, she can't stay in the house for ever!'

Aunt Kitty gently touched Ava's arm. 'We'll put her in the utility room first, so she can get used to moving around and being on her own. If it's all going well, we'll pop her out in the back barn.'

Ava relaxed a little. If Hope was just going to be in the utility room for now, she wouldn't be far away.

'You can help me set everything up, if you like, Ava,' said Aunt Kitty. 'To make sure it's just right.'

Ava nodded as her aunt got up from the table.

'No time like the present. I'll see you in there,'

she said, disappearing from the kitchen.

Ava looked at Hope. Uncle John was right – the cardboard box wasn't much good for her now that she could stand. Soon she'd be able to get out, and the kitchen wasn't the best place for her to wander around! Ava picked up the box with Hope in it. As she leaned over, Hope raised her head and her nose touched Ava's for a moment. Her heart skipped.

'Did you see that?' she asked excitedly, turning to look at her uncle and cousin, who were finishing their lunch at the table.

Uncle John smiled at her.

'She likes you. No wonder, with how you've been looking after her.'

Ava smiled back, and she carried Hope into the utility room. Aunt Kitty appeared with an armful of bits and bobs.

'Shove those work boots to the side there, Ava. Make some room in the middle.'

Aunt Kitty began unfolding a makeshift pen. She opened it until it made a complete circle.

'This is an old puppy pen,' said Aunt Kitty, securing the ends. 'It'll give Hope some more space but also make sure she doesn't cause any mischief!'

'What's that?' asked Ava, pointing to something by Aunt Kitty's feet.

'A heat-lamp,' she replied, holding it up.

It looked like a large industrial light fitting: a bulb with a domed metal shade and a long chain attached to the top. Aunt Kitty reached up to hook the chain

over a screw in the wooden ceiling beam. The lamp was now hanging down inside Hope's new pen.

Tom appeared, carrying an armful of straw. He spread it out in the pen so there was a thin layer all over.

'It's not the first time we've done this, Ava,' said Aunt Kitty with a reassuring smile. 'Right. Pop Hope in and then we'll check the lamp. Give her the blanket too so she has something familiar.'

Ava gently placed Hope in the pen and watched as she sniffed the straw. To Ava's delight, Hope skipped happily around.

'She likes it!' Ava beamed.

'Course she does,' said Tom.

He reached across to switch on the plug. A soft, warm glow from the heat-lamp lit up the golden straw below.

'Check the heat, Ava,' said Aunt Kitty, gesturing at the lamp.

Ava leaned over the waist-height pen and nudged her hand into the orange glow.

'That's really warm!' said Ava. 'I thought Hope was going to miss the heat from the oven, but that's perfect!'

'It's like a warm summer's day,' said Aunt Kitty wistfully.

'Right. There's a few more jobs in the lambing shed – then we're done for the day,' said Uncle John, appearing behind them and handing Tom and Ava their coats.

Ava paused in the doorway. She looked back at Hope, still skipping in her new pen.

'Don't worry – I'll keep an eye on Hope,' said Aunt Kitty with a smile.

'I'll be back to do your bottle, Hope,' Ava called, before heading outside.

Ava had just finished giving Hope her teatime milk when Tom came to fetch his boots.

'You off somewhere again?' asked Ava, looking up from the pen.

'Just doing the last checks of the day,' he replied, grabbing his coat.

'I can do it,' offered Ava, jumping up from the floor. She saw Tom hesitate. 'Please, Tom. I'm trying to do my bit. I really want to help while I'm here.'

'We can do it together, if you like?' suggested Tom.

Ava felt torn. Part of her would have loved to do it with Tom, but the other part really wanted to prove herself to him. He was just starting to trust her, and maybe if she did this by herself, he'd respect her even more.

'I'm sure I can manage on my own. I've seen what you normally do, and you said yourself that I've been doing a good job with Hope.'

Tom sighed. 'Okay, fine. I guess you have done

well with Hope. And you've been a real help the last few days.'

Ava smirked.

'What?' asked Tom.

'That's the first time you've called her by her name.'

'Is it?'

'Yep!' said Ava. 'Maybe you're starting to like her?'

'Maybe.' Tom shrugged with the hint of a smile. 'Anyway, you better get going before it gets dark.'

After Tom had given her a quick reminder of the end-of-day routine, Ava headed outside. Her first job was to give Jet his tea. Tom had shown her how much to give him and sworn her to secrecy when he added the leftover beef he'd managed to smuggle from last night's dinner. Ava stayed a lot longer with the sheepdog than she'd meant to as he kept insisting on more tummy rubs.

Next on the list was Magpie the farm cat's dinner. Miraculously, she appeared out of nowhere as soon as Ava opened the pouch of food – just as Tom said she would. She gave Magpie a quick stroke before moving on to the sheep check.

The hill sheep had already been done earlier that afternoon, so Ava went down to the lambing shed to check on the day's newborns and their mothers before casting her eye over the sheep in the fields in front of the farmhouse. As everything had been quiet so far, Ava decided to make a detour to see Harris. The old Shetland pony had made his way to the fence to greet her by the time she arrived. Ava held out her hand, wondering if it was polite to let him sniff it and accept her like she'd done with Jet. Harris nudged her hand, and Ava thought he might be hoping she had a carrot for him.

'Sorry, Harris. No treats tonight.'

She ran her hand gently down the side of his

neck, smoothing his rough, wiry mane.

'Next time though – I promise.'

Ava stood stroking Harris for a little while longer in the fading light. This was the closest she'd ever been to a pony, and Harris radiated calm, even if he could be a bit grumpy. Ava found him utterly fascinating. Once Harris had decided there was definitely no carrot coming, he sauntered away across the field. Ava suddenly felt very tired and stifled a yawn – it had been another busy but rewarding day, working on the farm.

As Ava trudged wearily back up the farm track, she yawned again. She'd hardly had any sleep the last couple of nights, what with waking up to feed Hope. Ava suddenly couldn't wait to get back to the warm farmhouse and kick off her wellies. The chickens were the last job to do, and then she'd be done.

It was almost dusk as Ava reached the chicken

barn and most of the chickens had gone back inside as Tom said they did every night. Ava thought it was amazing that the chickens put themselves to bed! She yawned again as she rounded up a few stragglers in the field and guided them into the barn. As the last chicken strutted through the door, Ava's pocket began to vibrate. She took out her phone and her face lit up as she read the caller's name.

'Mum!' she breathed into the phone.

The answer crackled back at her.

'Mum, can you hear me?'

Ava checked her phone – there was barely any reception.

'Hang on, Mum. I'm going to get a better position – don't hang up.'

Ava raced towards the farmhouse.

'Mum? Can you hear me?'

Her mum's voice was now crystal clear and she could hear her dad too. In that moment, she realized just how much she'd missed them. Hope had kept her so busy, she'd been distracted, but now, she couldn't stop the tears from flowing.

'Hi, Ava, love. How's it going on the farm?'

'Oh, you know,' said Ava, not quite sure where to begin. 'It's just different.'

'Good different or bad different?' asked Ava's mum, sounding concerned.

'I'm enjoying it more than I thought I would,' said Ava honestly. 'I saw a lamb being born, which was amazing! I helped Tom clean out the chickens . . . which wasn't as amazing. I've collected eggs, fed the dog, made friends with Harris the Shetland pony. But best of all, I've rescued a lamb! She's called Hope!'

Ava heard her parents laughing softly.

'Sounds busy,' said her dad. 'Everyone else okay? Are they looking after you well?'

'Tom's being his usual annoying self and bossing me about, but I'm learning lots.'

'Well, he does know more about the farm than you,' replied her dad.

'Anyway, how's Chicago?' asked Ava, changing the subject. 'Have you had pancakes for breakfast yet?'

'Of course!' said her dad.

'And how's the job? Are you going to save the world with your brand-new super antibiotic that makes everyone better?'

'Ha ha. Maybe,' said her mum.

Ava's parents talked excitedly about their work so far, how lovely their American colleagues were and how nice the hotel was. It was so good to finally speak to them. Ava really missed her parents, despite being happier at the farm than she thought she would be. They stayed on the phone until Ava couldn't keep her eyes open any more.

'Night-night, Mum. Night-night, Dad.'

'Goodnight, love. We'll be back before you know it,' said her mum.

As Ava headed inside the farmhouse, her heart felt full. She smiled at Hope, fast asleep in her pen. But as she looked more closely, her smile faltered. Something was missing. Ava burst into the kitchen.

'Where's my sleeping bag?'

'I've put it upstairs. You can't sleep with her for ever, Ava,' explained Aunt Kitty.

'But she'll miss me.'

'Maybe.' Aunt Kitty shrugged. 'But she'll miss you even more when you go home if you've kept her company every night.'

Ava sighed. Aunt Kitty did have a point and, besides, she was far too tired to argue. She'd enjoyed sleeping next to Hope, and Ava knew she couldn't do it for ever, but it was over more quickly than she'd expected.

'Why don't you get an early night, sweetheart. I can do Hope's bottle later.'

'No, it's fine. I'll wake up to do it. But I think I'll head to bed – I am pretty zonked.'

'Okay, sweetheart. But let me know if it gets too much – I'm here to help.'

'Will do, Aunt Kitty. Night-night.'

'Oh, and, Ava,' called Aunt Kitty as Ava reached the stairs. 'Thanks for checking on everything tonight.'

Ava smiled as she trudged up to her room wearily. It felt good to be useful. Her smile widened at the thought of getting into her warm bed.

# Chapter Nine

# THE ESCAPE

Ava woke with a start in the middle of the night – her phone alarm was vibrating on the bedside table, the screen illuminating a small pocket of light in the darkness. She grabbed the edge of her duvet and flung it open – Hope was downstairs and she needed Ava. The cold air was an unwelcome shock from the warmth of snuggling under the cover moments before.

'Ugh!' she muttered, flicking the duvet back

across her. It had been warm in the kitchen in front of the oven, and she hadn't minded getting up to do Hope's bottle then. Ava stuck one foot out from under the quilt, deciding a slow and steady approach was best. She nudged the rest of her leg out, letting the cold air envelop it. This way wasn't any better.

'Come on, Ava,' she whispered to herself.

Ava gritted her teeth and forced herself out of bed. She grabbed her hoodie from the floor and pulled it over her head. Ava stepped towards the door but stopped, looking down at her bare feet. They were warm enough now, but she knew the stone floor downstairs would feel like a glacier. She put on a discarded sock she found on top of the chest of drawers and looked for the other.

She switched on her phone's torch, afraid if she turned on the bedroom light, it might wake someone else in the house. Ava scanned the room, trying to locate the missing sock amongst the mess on her bedroom floor – her mum was always complaining she was too untidy at home! She spotted a dark lump under the window.

'Yes!' she whispered.

Ava tiptoed to the window and grabbed the sock. Leaning against the windowsill, she balanced precariously on one leg and slipped it on. The thin, flowery curtains were slightly ajar and something outside caught Ava's eye. She pulled the curtains apart a little more and squinted into the darkness. At the end of the farm track, a small torchlike beam was bobbing around. It was a few metres along from the main farm gate. Ava listened to the house, making out the gentle snores of her uncle. She frowned. It wasn't Uncle John out there, and she didn't think it would be Aunt Kitty either. Tom would be in trouble if he sneaked out at this time of night, so who was it?

Ava looked out of the window again into total

darkness. She scoured the area she'd seen the light moving, but it had vanished. Ava yawned and rubbed her eyes. Had she dreamed it? Maybe her tired eyes were playing tricks on her.

Ava slipped out of her bedroom, opening the door as quietly as she could – she hoped the little squeak it made wouldn't wake anyone. She crept down the creaky wooden stairs and into the kitchen. The heat from the oven welcomed Ava and she wished Hope was still in front of it. Instead, Magpie the farm cat was curled up where the lamb used to be. She opened one amber eye to look at Ava, before closing it again to go back to sleep. Ava made her way through the kitchen, her socked feet silent on the tiled floor. She opened the door of the utility room and gasped – the pen was empty!

'Hope?' Ava whispered.

But there was no sign of the lamb, only ruffled straw and Hope's blanket.

'Hope?' said Ava again, her heart pounding in her chest.

A sudden movement to her right made Ava jump. She leaped backwards as the row of coats hanging on the wall rippled. Ava took a deep breath and stepped towards the coats. A sneeze from behind

Uncle John's wax jacket caught her by surprise.

*Baaa.*

Ava jumped again as Hope skipped out from her hiding place.

'Oh, Hope!' cried Ava, clasping her chest. 'You scared the life out of me! How did you get out of your pen?'

*Baa.*

Hope strutted over to Ava, and she could see how much stronger and steadier the lamb was getting. Hope nuzzled into Ava's legs.

'I know you're hungry and I'm late, but I need to get you back in your pen before Aunt Kitty finds out.'

Ava inspected the makeshift pen. It was too high for Hope to have jumped over, so Ava grasped it, pushing and pulling to see if there was a weak spot.

'Aha,' she said triumphantly.

One of the clips connecting the flimsy metal

sections had come off, leaving a lamb-sized gap in the middle. It wouldn't have been too difficult for a determined Hope to break through. Ava connected the two ends of the pen back together.

'Try and get through that now,' Ava said to Hope.

She picked up the lamb, pulling her in for a quick cuddle. Hope's fleece was thicker and curlier now, and Ava thought she didn't feel as thin either. Hope's body was warm and comforting, and it almost felt like Hope was leaning in to get closer.

*Baa.*

'All right, all right. I'll get your milk.'

Ava put Hope back into her pen and began making up the bottle. Now she was older, Hope was on a different powdered milk, but it still had to be made up fresh and given to her regularly. Moments later, Ava climbed over the pen and knelt on the straw beside Hope. The lamb sniffed the warm bottle for a moment before hungrily taking it in her mouth and gulping the milk. Ava tipped the bottle up, remembering to make sure the lamb didn't take in too much air while drinking so she didn't get a windy tummy.

The door to the utility creaked softly and Ava looked up to see a sleepy Aunt Kitty.

'Okay, sweetheart?'

'All good, thanks, Aunt Kitty,' replied Ava, wondering if she should tell her about Hope escaping.

'I didn't hear you get up.'

'I tried not to wake you,' whispered Ava.

'Thank you, sweetheart. If you need a break from the night-time feeds, just let me know. I know it's the holidays and you don't have school, but I saw how tired you were tonight.'

'Thanks, Aunt Kitty, but I'm okay.'

Ava stroked Hope, who was nibbling on her hoodie.

'Don't be too long,' said Aunt Kitty with a yawn.

'I won't. I'll stay with her for a bit, then head back up to bed,' replied Ava, tickling Hope's chin.

Aunt Kitty smiled.

'She's coming on really well, Ava. You should be proud of yourself.'

Ava felt her cheeks flush with Aunt Kitty's compliment. She couldn't help but smile — she was finally starting to feel like part of the Whistledown Farm family.

# Chapter Ten

# THE ATTACK

Ava's bedroom door flew open.

'What did you do?' shouted Tom.

Ava blinked her eyes against the bright morning light.

'W-what?'

'You were supposed to check everything last night!'

Ava pushed herself up in bed as her eyes focused on Tom's face. His eyes were dark and blazing –

his whole body was shaking.

'I . . . I . . . don't know what you mean,' stammered Ava.

'Did you check everything was safe last night?'

'Yes!'

'Did you do the chickens too?'

'Yes – I made sure they all went in the barn.'

'And then what?'

'And then I . . . I don't know what you're asking, Tom?'

'Did you check they were shut in properly?'

Ava frowned and rubbed her eyes. Her mind was still hazy with sleep, and Tom shouting at her wasn't helping.

'You can't remember, can you?'

Tom stormed out of her room, his feet stomping loudly down the stairs. Ava hesitated for a moment as confusion clouded her head. Snapping into action, she leaped out of bed, a feeling of dread sweeping through her. Ava yanked on some clothes as she stumbled down the stairs, forcing herself to wake up properly. She could hear Tom and Uncle John's raised voices. As she pushed the kitchen door open, they fell silent. Tom turned away from her, but Ava caught a glimpse of his face. He was crying.

'I don't understand what's going on,' said Ava. 'What's happened?'

Tom spun round to face her.

'You're what's happened!'

The full heat of his anger was directed at her, forcing her to take a step back.

'Everything was fine before you got here!'

Tom ran out of the kitchen, leaving Uncle John and Ava standing in an uncomfortable silence.

'Uncle John, I don't know what I've done wrong.'

His hands were on his hips as he looked at her. He sighed, then spoke quietly.

'Ava, love, did you check the chickens were in last night?'

'Yes!'

'Did you check the barn door was closed and locked properly? And that the gate to the field was shut?'

'Yes, I . . .'

Ava stopped. She remembered shooing the chickens into the barn and taking hold of the door. That's when her phone had rung. She'd run off to get better reception. Ava's stomach plummeted. She felt queasy.

'Oh no! Mum and Dad rang and maybe I . . . maybe I didn't lock the door! Or shut the gate!'

Her uncle's shoulders sagged.

'Why? What's happened?' asked Ava. 'I'm really sorry, Uncle John. Surely it doesn't matter for one night?'

'It does matter, Ava.' Uncle John's voice was quiet.

Ava frowned.

'Are the chickens okay?'

Uncle John hesitated and Ava didn't like the look on his face. Without waiting for his answer, she sped out of the farmhouse, grabbing her wellies on the way.

'Ava, wait! Don't . . .'

She didn't hang around to hear what else he was going to say. She ran through the courtyard towards the chicken barn and field. She skidded to a halt at the open gate. Aunt Kitty was standing in the field with her arms round Tom, and Ava tried to take in the devastation surrounding them. There were feathers *everywhere*.

Aunt Kitty looked up and her eyes widened as she saw Ava standing there. Tom lifted his head and glared at her, his face wet with tears.

Tom ran past her, knocking Ava against the stone wall. She stared after him in confusion, watching him head down to the hay shed. All at once, Aunt Kitty was by her side, turning her gently towards the house.

'Go back to the farmhouse, Ava.'

Ava shrugged her off.

'But I don't understand! What's happened?'

Aunt Kitty sighed.

'A fox got into the chickens last night, Ava.'

'Are they okay?'

'No, Ava, they're not. Quite a few have been killed.'

Ava's stomach somersaulted.

'Because of me?' Ava's eyes widened in horror.

Ava pushed past her aunt and went into the feather-covered field. She stood in the middle, trying to take in what had happened.

Ava felt Aunt Kitty's arm round her.

'How many are left?' she asked, her voice quiet and small.

'Only a handful,' replied Aunt Kitty, her voice trembling.

Ava began to sob and buried her face into her aunt's shoulder.

'I'm so sorry.'

Aunt Kitty held her while she cried. Ava wished she was anywhere else but Whistledown Farm.

'But the fox hasn't even eaten them!' wailed Ava.

Aunt Kitty sighed. 'Sometimes a fox will just take one or two to feed her hungry cubs, but sometimes . . . Well, sometimes some foxes just cause havoc.'

'Tom's never going to speak to me again, is he?'

'Give him time, sweetheart. He raised a lot of these chickens himself.'

Ava gasped.

'HB? Loki?'

Aunt Kitty gently shook her head.

'We can't find Loki, but we did find HB. She didn't make it.'

'No!' cried Ava.

She ran to the barn and ducked inside the open chicken door. This was all her fault. No wonder Tom was so angry with her. She felt Aunt Kitty behind her.

'Tom will just need some time.'

'He'll never forgive me,' muttered Ava, tears falling down her face.

'He will. Tom knows well enough where there's livestock, there'll also be dead stock. These things happen, Ava. That's why we do what we can to protect the animals we have. There's no such thing as a small job on a farm. Maybe we didn't explain that well enough.'

'I was so tired and I . . . I wasn't concentrating properly. Then Mum and Dad rang and I just . . . I just . . .'

Ava sobbed. She knew her parents would tell her to try and make it up to Tom, to tell him she was sorry. She ran out of the chicken barn as fast as her wellies would carry her, down to the hay shed.

'Tom?'

She looked at the bales of hay stacked on top of each other. She couldn't see him.

'Tom, are you there?'

Her voice echoed round the enormous space. Ava listened, trying to work out where Tom was. A gentle spring breeze swirled round her as the birds sang in the trees, but there was no sign of Tom.

'I'm sorry, Tom. It was an accident.'

'Go away, Ava!'

The venom in Tom's voice struck Ava hard.

'Please, Tom. I'm so sorry about HB.'

There was a deathly silence from the hay bales.

'Tom, I just want you to know I feel terrible.'

'Get lost, Ava. My chickens would still be alive if it wasn't for you!' Tom's face appeared over a bale. 'No one wants you here, Ava. They never did.

You're useless. Just go home and don't come back!'

Tom's face disappeared and Ava could hear his muffled sobs. What did he mean they didn't want her here? She turned and ran away from the hay shed. Tears were rolling down her face as she tugged open the field gate. She dashed through and slammed the gate shut behind her, hearing it click into place.

She stared at it. At least that was one less thing they'd be angry about. Uncle John had spent at least fifteen minutes yesterday impressing on her how important it was to shut gates so the animals didn't get out. But he hadn't said anything about shutting gates to stop other animals getting *in*. Her cheeks burned at the thought of them not wanting her on the farm. Had her mum and dad begged them to have her?

Ava ran across to the opposite side of the field and climbed over an old stile in the fence. She slumped on a damp grey rock beside a small fast-running stream on the other side and watched it dance down the gentle slope of the hillside. Ava wished with all her heart she could run away with the water. How could she have been so careless? Just as she was beginning to be part of the farm and prove herself, she'd let everybody down.

# Chapter Eleven

# THE WOODS

Ava wiped her face on her sleeve. She'd stopped crying, but her eyes felt tired and sore. The sound of an engine in the farm's woodlands carried towards her on the wind. It didn't sound like the vehicle Uncle John used around the farm; it was smoother, more like a normal car. Ava stood and scanned the treeline, trying to make something out. Everyone else was up at the farm, dealing with the aftermath of the fox attack, so who could be in the woods?

The engine stopped. Ava squinted across the shadowy woodland again, trying to see if she could catch the tiniest glimpse of the source of the noise. Further along from where she thought the sound had been coming from, a figure emerged from the trees, startling her. She couldn't see their face as the hood of their sweatshirt was pulled up high. They stepped towards the fence-line, giving the rails a shake.

The figure disappeared back into the trees and Ava scanned for any sign of movement. The figure popped out again a few metres up the fence-line, this time much closer. Ava felt on edge. She didn't think this person was supposed to be there. She glanced over her shoulder towards the farmhouse beyond. It was quite a way to go and get help, and what if this was a totally normal visitor? She didn't want to cause any more drama today.

The figure melted into the trees again. Ava stepped towards the woods but froze as the figure re-emerged, this time at the field gate directly in front of her. They were still quite far away and hadn't noticed her yet. Ava's mind raced – what would Uncle John do? Her mum's warnings about not talking to strangers echoed loudly in her head. Ava was determined to make amends for her disastrous mistake last night though. She couldn't just do *nothing*.

Ava took a deep breath and walked towards the figure, eyes fixed on their dark trousers and green hoodie. She was still a fair distance away but close enough to see it was a man of a similar size and build to Uncle John . . . but it definitely *wasn't* Uncle John. She stopped. Ava glanced behind her, checking she had a clear route in case she needed to run. The man looked up, his eyes widening in surprise at the sight of Ava.

'Can I help you?' shouted Ava, hoping her voice sounded strong and confident.

'All good,' said the man.

He turned away from her so she couldn't see his face.

'Just looking for my dog. Darn thing ran off after a squirrel.'

'Do you want me to get my aunt and uncle? Maybe we can all look together?'

She dug her shaking hands into her pockets.

'Nah. Doesn't look like it's here.'

The man turned back towards the trees.

'What does it look like?' shouted Ava.

'What does what look like?' said the man, keeping his back to her.

'Your dog?'

'Oh, yeah. German shepherd. Big one. Don't go looking for it – it'll take your hand off!'

The man vanished into the shadows between the trees. Ava stood where she was, knowing it would be silly to follow. Either the man was up to no good or there was actually a scary dog lurking in the woods. The engine started up again and Ava could hear the vehicle driving away. The sound grew fainter until it disappeared altogether. Ava stood alone in the field, staring at the dense woodland beyond the fence. She knew she should tell someone about the man, but what would she say? He hadn't *actually* done anything wrong. Maybe he *had* been looking for his dog.

Ava was torn. She didn't want to go back to the farmyard yet. She felt awful about the fox attack, and about what Tom had said that no one wanted her at Whistledown in the first place. But she had the same feeling in her gut about the man in the woods as when she'd seen the light out of her bedroom window in the night. Ava's breath caught as she realized she'd forgotten to tell anyone about the light in the awful commotion of the morning. But maybe the light was perfectly normal and so was the person in the woods? After all, there was *so much* she didn't know about the farm; last night had proved that. Ava sighed. She wasn't cut out for farm life and wished she was back at home, snuggled up on the sofa in her house without an animal in sight.

Ava walked away from the woods, not daring to glance behind her in case the man came back. She suddenly felt nervous and wanted to put distance between her and the trees. She needed to clear her head too. Ava made her way up the field, following a similar path to the day she'd found Hope. Only a few days had passed, but it seemed much longer – so much had happened.

A bird circled high above her, and Ava shielded her eyes against the spring sun, watching it soar. She wished she knew what kind of bird it was. Ava could see it was big with a forked tail. She made a mental note to ask Tom. Her stomach flipped – she'd forgotten he wasn't speaking to her.

Ava yomped up the hillside, pushing thoughts about Tom from her mind. She felt something banging against her leg and plunged her hand into her pocket. It was her phone.

'Mum. Dad,' she breathed.

They'd know what she should do! Ava called them, pressing the phone to her ear. The international dial tone stopped as it clicked to voicemail. She closed her eyes, willing away the tears that were threatening to fall yet again. Ava realized she would have to figure this out on her own. She looked towards the woodland. *Of course* she had to tell someone about the man. She'd already made one mistake and didn't want to make another, otherwise they *really* wouldn't want her there.

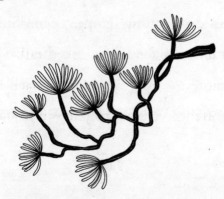

# Chapter Twelve

# HOPE'S BARN

Ava burst into the farmhouse. Aunt Kitty was in the utility room and jumped in surprise at Ava's entrance.

'Aunt Kitty, I need to tell you . . .'

Ava stopped mid-sentence as she realized Aunt Kitty was dismantling Hope's pen. She looked around frantically for Hope, but she was nowhere to be seen.

'Where is she? Where's Hope? What's happened?'

All thoughts of the man in the woods and the strange night-time light were replaced with an anxious worry for Hope.

'It's okay, don't panic, she's fine, Ava. Nothing's happened to her. She just needs to be out of the house,' said Aunt Kitty, putting the makeshift pen aside.

'What do you mean?' asked Ava, her face flushed.

'I came back and found her skipping about the kitchen.'

'Oh,' said Ava.

'Left little *presents* everywhere too.' Aunt Kitty smiled as she raised her eyebrows.

Ava frowned for a moment before she twigged what Aunt Kitty meant.

'Oh! Sorry, Aunt Kitty. Do you want me to clear it up?' asked Ava apologetically. She felt guilty that she hadn't told Aunt Kitty about Hope's escape last night.

'It's all done. You can help set everything up outside though. I've put her in the barn across from the chickens. If she's escaped once, she'll do it again, and I don't want her causing trouble in the house.'

Aunt Kitty unhooked the heat-lamp and passed it to Ava. They headed outside towards the barns in silence, Ava still wondering if she should confess about Hope's previous escape. She avoided looking at the chicken barn as it came into view. She knew it would be all cleaned up by now, but she couldn't bear to see the handful of chickens that were left. Guilt weighed heavily on her chest.

Aunt Kitty opened the door of the back barn, and Ava realized she hadn't ventured in there yet. She'd been in the storage barn, the chicken barn and the little one that housed bags of feed. This building was similar in size to the chicken barn, with the same whitewashed walls and concrete floor, but it was empty.

120

'What's this used for?' asked Ava.

'Whatever we need, really,' said Aunt Kitty. 'It can be an overflow for extra feed, a makeshift nursery or temporary storage. Harris has spent a couple of harsh winters in here too.'

Ava gazed around the barn. From what she knew of the temperamental Shetland pony, she'd guess he would like it here.

'This way,' called Aunt Kitty.

Ava followed her aunt through an old wooden door, dotted with peeling patches of paint. She realized it must have once been a beautiful bright shade of blue. It reminded her of a mural of the sea in the park back in the city. Ava tried to push away thoughts of home.

*Baa.*

'Hope!'

Ava's worry about Hope vanished as she saw the little lamb sitting on a fresh bed of straw.

'Hmm,' said Aunty Kitty. 'Looks like butter wouldn't melt now. But we know better, you little escape artist.'

*Baa.*

Aunt Kitty and Ava set the heat-lamp at the perfect height for Hope to nestle under. Ava felt uncomfortable working with her aunt for the first time since coming here. She felt terrible about the chickens and about Hope making a mess in the kitchen. Tom's words were still going round and round in her head too. Aunt Kitty had made her feel so welcome, but it must have all been for show.

'Perfect,' said Aunt Kitty. 'She'll be safe and sound in here tonight.'

Ava looked down at Hope, who seemed smaller somehow, more vulnerable in the barn. An awful thought crept into Ava's mind.

'Will she be okay in here? What if a fox gets her too?'

'Honestly, she'll be fine in here, sweetheart.'

Ava winced at the word 'sweetheart'. It sounded so forced now Ava knew the truth.

'But the house is so far away. How will we know if something's wrong?'

'It's perfectly safe in here, Ava. The walls are thick stone and there's two doors to get through.'

'I need to stay with her!' shouted Ava.

Her words sounded fierce, filled with the burning resentment she suddenly felt towards her aunt. 'I'm going to stay with her tonight, Aunt Kitty, and you can't stop me.'

Ava glared at her aunt, but inside she was panicking. She'd never spoken to anyone like this before, let alone Aunt Kitty. She may not be welcome at Whistledown Farm, but if she had to be here, then she was going to do it her way. She would protect Hope no matter what, just like she'd promised.

'Lambs are normally out in the fields, Ava,'

said Aunt Kitty coolly.

'But she's all alone! Hope's been abandoned! She doesn't have anyone to look after her. I'm her only friend!'

Hot, angry tears had begun to flow. Aunt Kitty took a step forward and opened her arms, but Ava stepped back. A flicker of hurt crossed her aunt's face, and Ava looked down at the straw. She heard Aunt Kitty sigh.

'Fine. You can stay with her tonight if it means that much to you.'

Ava sniffed and wiped her face with her sleeve.

Aunt Kitty lowered her voice.

'I care about keeping Hope safe too, Ava. She's very special. You both are.'

Ava glared at her aunt. In her head, she shouted, *Liar!* But she couldn't bring herself to say it. Instead, she fixed her eyes on Hope.

The door to the barn opened and Uncle John

appeared, breaking the tension.

'I could do with a hand in the lambing shed, Ava. Tom was going to help, but . . .'

Ava bit her lip. Maybe some time in there would be good.

The warmth of the lambing shed enveloped Ava, and the sight of the newborn lambs melted her turbulent feelings away.

'We've had quite a few more lambs today,' said Uncle John.

Sure enough, several sheep had tiny newborns with them, and Ava remembered Aunt Kitty's words about there being life *and* death on a farm. The life part was magical.

'What can I help with?' asked Ava.

'I'm pleased you asked,' said Uncle John, handing her a spray can.

Ava frowned.

'What's this for?'

'How's your handwriting, Ava?' asked Uncle John with a grin.

He walked over to the smaller pens.

'When the sheep have their lambs, they're put into their own individual pens. As you can see, they're all full. These little families are ready to go out to make room for the new lambs.'

'Okay,' said Ava. 'But I still don't understand what the spray can is for?'

'Aha!' said Uncle John. 'Follow me!'

He led Ava outside towards the large field behind the lambing shed. He stopped by the gate and pointed.

'*That's* what we use the spray for.'

Ava saw that each sheep had a number on their fleece, written in bright blue spray. The lambs had matching numbers on theirs.

'It's special sheep-marker spray. If we number the

sheep and lambs, we can keep track of how many we've had and which lambs belong to which sheep. Sometimes the mothers and lambs can get separated, so numbering them means we can quickly match them up again.'

Ava smiled.

'Simple yet effective!' said Uncle John, walking away.

'And you want me to write the numbers on?' asked Ava, jogging to keep up with her uncle.

'Yep!'

Back in the lambing shed, Ava stood by the nearest pen, sheep marker at the ready.

'Just spray the number on the side of the sheep. This one should be twenty-two.'

Ava swallowed. She reached towards the sheep with a shaky hand.

'What if I mess it up?' she asked quietly, her mouth dry.

Uncle John laughed. 'You can't mess it up. Whatever you put on that sheep, we'll just put the same on the lambs. In fact, seeing as it's your first one, why don't you write your initial?'

'Really?' said Ava, her eyes widening with excitement.

'Why not?' her uncle said with a shrug.

Ava gently pressed down on the nozzle, moving her hand steadily as the blue letter *A* took shape on the white fleece. Ava stood back and admired her handiwork.

'Perfect,' said Uncle John, sounding impressed.

Ava had to admit it was a neat job. Uncle John leaned into the pen and picked up the lambs.

'Now these two,' he said, holding them up for Ava.

It was a bit trickier to write on the smaller lambs,

but Ava managed a couple of perfectly formed *A*s.

'Now you'll never get lost,' whispered Ava. It made her think of Hope and how they'd found each other. Ava looked around the lambing shed, bursting with new life. Despite what had happened this morning, she felt lucky to be here.

'Shall we keep going?' suggested Uncle John, who was already moving to the next pen.

Ava and her uncle continued numbering the sheep and lambs. When they were all done, they let them out into the field, and Ava watched happily as the lambs explored their new home.

Ava kept herself busy for the rest of the morning in the lambing shed, forgetting all about the fox and the man in the woods. She loved picking up the new lambs and carrying them to their own pens, getting their mothers to follow – they went anywhere their lambs did. She refilled the water buckets and made sure the sheep had plenty of hay. Ava was almost out of jobs when Aunt Kitty arrived.

'Why don't we head inside for some lunch? You must be hungry,' she suggested. 'Can you go and get Tom? I think he's still in the hay shed.'

Ava's stomach twisted. The thought of Tom brought her crashing back to reality and all the morning's horrible feelings came flooding back.

'Get him yourself,' said Ava, fighting back tears as she ran towards the house.

# Chapter Thirteen

# THE SLEEPOVER

Tom was nowhere to be seen at lunchtime, and Ava ate alone in her bedroom, deciding to stay there for the rest of the day.

Her room at the farm was cosy and, although it wasn't her own blue-painted bedroom that she'd helped decorate back home, she liked it nonetheless. She'd spent the afternoon sitting on her windowsill, staring out across the fields. Ava had opened the window a little, and she felt a cool breeze envelop her in little gusty waves. She was surprised to find she missed being outside.

Everywhere was green, a colour Ava wasn't used to seeing much at home. Spring had touched the trees and fields as far as the eye could see, with sprinkles of yellow daffodils puncturing the vast ocean of lush green shades. Ava couldn't remember the last time she'd just sat still. Normally, she'd be heading to an after-school club or completing a weekend of jam-packed activities. Life was so busy at home, and here . . . well, here was busy with farm work, but it had a different flow. Uncle John had described it as 'the pace of nature', and Ava couldn't agree more.

Ava stayed on the windowsill looking out over the farm until Harris was lost to the gloom of dusk and her skin was peppered with goosebumps. She reluctantly closed the window and sat on the end of her bed. A tantalizing smell wafted up the stairs, but

Ava didn't think she could face them all. She still had another week to endure before her parents flew home, and it felt like an eternity now.

A loud knock made Ava jump. Uncle John's face appeared round her bedroom door.

'Your aunt's made steak and ale pie for tea and she's gone to a lot of trouble. Tom will be in soon, so I expect to see you downstairs for dinner too.'

He locked eyes with Ava for a few seconds before disappearing, leaving her door open. The smell of pie and chips intensified and Ava's stomach rumbled. She swung her legs over the bed and sat there for a moment to think. Ava couldn't face playing happy families at the dinner table. She still felt guilty about the fox, and the embarrassment about no one wanting her at Whistledown made her feel even worse. The sleeping bag crumpled on the floor caught her eye and she instantly knew what she was going to do.

Ava ran down the stairs and into the kitchen, her sleeping bag tucked under one arm. Trying not to lose her nerve, she quickly grabbed her plate of food from the table where the rest of the family were sat waiting and headed out of the door before anyone could stop her. Ava marched over to Hope's barn, trying not to spill anything. She fumbled with the various barn latches, which weren't so easy to negotiate with her arms full.

Once inside, Ava let out a deep breath. She couldn't believe she'd just done that. She dumped her sleeping bag on the straw and sat against the stone wall with her dinner plate on her lap. She stared at the food and sighed. In her haste to leave, she hadn't picked up a knife and fork.

*Baa.*

Ava looked up to see Hope sitting contentedly under the heat-lamp. She felt herself relax a little.

*Baa.*

134

'I know, I know. Next time I need to think it through properly. I didn't get a drink either!'

*Baa.*

Ava smiled. She'd never been a rebel before. If her mum and dad could see her now, sitting on a barn floor eating steak pie, chips and gravy with her fingers, with a lamb for company, they wouldn't believe it either.

Ava finished most of her food and drank the leftover gravy from her plate. Through the small window in the barn, Ava could see darkness had descended outside, and a wave of tiredness washed over her. She checked the barn doors were closed, but could still feel a draught seeping in through the cracks. For a brief moment, she wished she was tucked up snugly in her warm bed.

*Baa.*

Ava looked at Hope under the soft orange glow of the heat-lamp and all thoughts of heading inside vanished.

'I'm here, Hope. There's no way that fox is getting in.'

She jiggled her way inside the sleeping bag. This is *exactly* where she wanted to be.

# Chapter Fourteen

# DARKNESS . . .

Ava woke to a pitch-black barn. She rubbed her eyes, trying to work out where she was. The rustle of straw jogged her memory.

'Hope,' she murmured.

Ava didn't understand why she couldn't see anything. She shivered, suddenly realizing the heat-lamp wasn't on.

Soft silvery moonlight seeped in through the barn window, allowing Ava to just make out Hope's dark silhouette. She reached out for her, and as Ava's fingers wove into Hope's soft black fleece, she gasped. Hope was freezing cold.

'No!' cried Ava. 'Hope!'

*Baa . . .*

Hope's bleat sounded weak and Ava's stomach flipped. She touched the lamp – it was stone cold! Ava wriggled out of her sleeping bag, beginning to panic. She stumbled over to the plug socket and desperately flicked the switch, but the lamp didn't turn on. Ava rushed back to pick up Hope, cradling the lamb tightly in her arms. She clumsily wriggled into the sleeping bag, holding a shivering Hope close to her. She rubbed the lamb's body, trying to warm her as quickly as possible.

*Baa.*

Ava stopped rubbing, but held Hope tightly against her – relieved to feel she had stopped shivering.

*Baa.*

Hope's bleats were muffled against Ava's chest, but she could have sworn they sounded stronger. Ava realized her vision was blurry and her cheeks were wet. She wasn't sure when she'd started crying, but now the tears were flowing, they wouldn't stop.

'Oh, Hope,' sobbed Ava. 'I don't know what I'd do if anything happened to you.'

She couldn't bear the thought of losing Hope, like Tom had lost HB and his other chickens.

'I . . . I don't feel lonely when I'm with you.'

Ava sniffed and stroked Hope under her chin.

*Baa.*

'You know what I'm talking about, don't you?'

*Baa.*

Ava smiled weakly.

'I know you don't really, but it *feels* like you do. I guess we're kind of the same. Neither of us really fits in anywhere. I thought I was starting to fit in here though.'

A large lump formed in Ava's throat as she remembered what Tom had said.

'They don't really want me on the farm,' Ava murmured to Hope. 'But you want me here, don't you?'

*Baa.*

The door to the barn creaked softly and Ava jumped. Torchlight flooded the darkness and Ava shielded her eyes from the blinding beam. She could make out a silhouette standing in the doorway – it was Aunt Kitty.

'I came to check on you,' said Aunt Kitty quietly. 'And to bring Hope this.'

She held out a bottle of milk. Aunt Kitty stepped forward and handed it to Ava before retreating back to the doorway.

'Thanks,' croaked Ava, wiping her face with her sleeve.

Ava gave Hope the bottle and she sucked on it

greedily, white froth growing at the corners of her mouth.

'How long were you there?' asked Ava.

'Long enough, sweetheart,' replied Aunt Kitty softly.

A heavy silence descended in the barn.

'Why do you think we don't want you here?' asked Aunt Kitty.

Ava felt a hot rage erupt inside her. 'Because you all hate me! And I hate you!'

Remorse washed over Ava instantly and she realized that she was angry with much more than just Aunt Kitty.

'You may hate me, Ava, but I definitely don't hate you,' said Aunt Kitty.

'But Tom said . . .'

Huge sobs racked Ava's body. She felt Aunt Kitty's warm arms round her, and Ava couldn't help but lean into them, giving in to their reassuring familiarity.

Ava wasn't sure how long they sat on the floor of the barn holding each other. But they stayed there until she'd stopped crying and her breathing was soft and regular. She pulled away and looked at Aunt Kitty in the gloom of the barn.

'I'm sorry, Aunt Kitty.'

Her aunt smiled sadly at her.

'I'm sorry too. I'm not sure what Tom said to you, but we very much want you here. We love you, sweetheart.'

Ava's lip trembled.

'He said no one wanted me here – you never did,' mumbled Ava.

'Well, that's absolutely not true. Tom was upset about the chickens and was probably just lashing out at you. Even if your parents weren't away, we'd love to have you stay at Whistledown. You're welcome here any time.'

Ava blinked back the tears again at the mention of her parents; she missed them so much her heart ached. She was proud of her mum and dad, and their important work, but she felt a bit jealous of it at times, especially when it took them away from her.

'They'll be back before you know it. They haven't abandoned you,' said Aunt Kitty knowingly.

Ava smiled weakly. 'It feels like they have.'

'They couldn't take you with them. You know that.'

'But they didn't ask me if I was okay with them going away.'

'It hasn't been that bad here, has it?' asked Aunt Kitty, concern in her eyes.

'No!' said Ava quickly. 'No offence, but I really didn't *want* to come. I thought I would hate it. But before this morning, the last few days were . . . well, I guess I can't remember the last time I felt that happy.'

'Oh, sweetheart,' said Aunt Kitty, pulling her in for another hug.

'I felt I finally belonged somewhere.' Ava bit her lip, knowing that she was about to admit something to Aunt Kitty that she'd never told anyone.

'It's hard back at home . . . I don't really have anyone to talk to. Mum and Dad work a lot and I don't have any proper friends any more, not since my best friend, Talia, moved away. I always feel like I don't fit in, but I didn't feel like that here until I messed it all up with the chickens. Tom was being nice to me too. Now he'll never forgive me.'

'He will. He just needs time. It was a shock. We

all know it was an accident.'

'I wouldn't forgive me if I were him.' Ava shuddered at the image of the feather-strewn chicken field.

*Baa.*

Ava looked at Hope. The lamb was now warm and energized, skipping around in the straw. Watching Hope made Ava's heart swell.

'Stopped working, has it?' asked Aunt Kitty, gesturing towards the heat-lamp.

Ava nodded.

'Well done for keeping Hope warm. Wait here.'

Aunt Kitty left to grab another heat-lamp. She replaced the broken one, then flicked the switch and a soft, reassuring glow flooded the small barn once again. Hope skipped towards it and immediately settled underneath.

An exhausted yawn escaped Ava – she felt wiped out.

'We should try and get some sleep,' said Aunt Kitty softly.

Ava nodded and settled herself in her sleeping bag.

'You going to be okay?' asked Aunt Kitty from the doorway.

'Yes, thanks, Aunt Kitty.'

'I'll be back in the morning with another bottle. You know where I am if you need me.'

Ava smiled at her aunt. 'I really am sorry. For everything.'

Aunt Kitty smiled back. 'I know, sweetheart. We love you, Ava. Sleep well.'

# Chapter Fifteen

# TEAMWORK

Ava entered the kitchen the next morning and was greeted by the smell of bacon and eggs. A knot formed in her stomach as she saw Tom talking to his mum. Ava took a deep breath – she had to face him sometime. Besides, she felt a little less terrible now she knew Tom had lied to her about no one wanting her at Whistledown Farm.

She headed into the kitchen and sat at the table. Tom didn't look up from his breakfast, but he didn't leave or shout at her either, which was progress in Ava's book. Ava glanced at Aunt Kitty, who was busy making a pot of tea. She wondered whether her aunt had told Tom she knew about his lie. There was no tension in the air, so she guessed she hadn't.

Uncle John breezed in, grabbing a cup of coffee.

'The tractor part I needed has arrived, so I'm off to pick it up. Everything's sorted in the lambing shed for now. I'll be back in a couple of hours!'

As she watched her uncle leave, Ava felt a bit disappointed that the lambing shed jobs had already been done. Her stomach rumbled. She started to make herself a bacon sandwich and reached out for the ketchup, but before she could grasp it, it was pulled away. She stared at Tom. He slowly opened the lid and squeezed some on his empty plate before theatrically closing the lid and placing the bottle on the table as far away from her as possible. Ava shrugged and picked up the brown sauce instead.

'I've got a lot to do today, so you're both going to have to help out,' said Aunt Kitty, turning to look at them. 'I need you to go down and shut the sheep out of the woodland. You can take Jet with you if you like.'

'I can do that on my own,' said Tom.

Aunt Kitty continued, 'Then, I'd like you *both* to check the woodland fencing.'

'Which bit?' asked Tom, his brow furrowing.

'All of it,' replied Aunt Kitty, taking a big drink of tea.

'All of it?' said Tom, eyes wide. 'But that'll take ages! I was going to hang out with my friends today!'

Aunt Kitty quietly sipped her tea, eyes fixed on her son.

'Maybe if we split up, we can get it done quicker?' suggested Tom.

He glanced at Ava — the first time he'd looked at her properly since the fox attack. Even she could tell

Aunt Kitty wasn't going to agree to that.

'I said –' Aunt Kitty narrowed her eyes at Tom – 'that I would like you both to do it. If there's broken fence wire, it will be much easier for the two of you to patch it up. Together.'

'But—'

'No discussion. Do it together. *Then* you can see your friends,' interrupted Aunt Kitty.

'Okay, Aunt Kitty,' said Ava.

The atmosphere in the warm kitchen had turned icy.

'*Okay, Aunt Kitty,*' mimicked Tom in an unflattering voice.

'Thomas!'

Tom stiffened at the use of his full name.

'I *will* check on your work later, and if I hear that there's been any arguments . . . there'll be big trouble. Do I make myself clear?'

'Yes,' Ava and her cousin both mumbled.

'Sorry? I didn't quite hear you?'

'Yes, Aunt Kitty.'

'Yes, Mum.'

Aunt Kitty walked out of the kitchen, leaving Tom and Ava sitting in an awkward silence. Ava risked a look at her cousin.

'I really am sorry, Tom.'

Tom stood up to leave.

'I liked the chickens – you know I did,' Ava said quietly.

Tom's face softened ever so slightly.

'It was an accident –' Ava sighed – 'I don't expect you to ever forgive me.'

Tom looked out the kitchen window, silent for a few moments.

'Come on,' he said finally. 'We better get going with Mum's ridiculous attempt to patch things up.'

Tom and Ava arrived at the woodland ten minutes later. Tom had walked a couple of metres in front of Ava, with Jet at his heel. She was out of breath, but she was determined not to fall behind. Tom turned to face her.

'Just do what I say. Don't do anything else. We all know how *that* turns out.'

Ava glared at him. Despite the cool spring air, she felt hot. Anger bubbled in her belly. It was like the first day all over again with him bossing her around. At least now she knew her aunt and uncle wanted her there, plus there was only a week until she went home.

Tom climbed over a gate, and Jet squeezed underneath, with Ava following close behind. She tried to keep up with her cousin as he strode through the woods, deftly manoeuvring round fallen branches and tufts of thick grass, all while carrying a heavy-looking bucket. Ava, however, hit every obstacle. She gritted her teeth, trying not to yelp at each trip, stumble or missed footing. Tom stopped by another wooden gate at the edge of the woods and thrust the bucket at Ava.

'Take this. Open the gate. Shake the bucket.'

Ava gave him a questioning look. Tom rolled his eyes.

'Shake the bucket and call the sheep. Jet and I will push them from behind. Just get out the way when they come through the gate.'

Tom walked into the woods, with Jet sticking close by his side.

'Come on, girls,' shouted Tom into the trees.

Ava watched Tom and Jet disappear between the trunks and into the gloom of the woodland.

Snapping into action, Ava unlatched the gate and tied it to the fence-line so it stayed open. She stood in the gap, feeling a mixture of excitement and nerves.

'Please don't mess up,' she whispered to herself.

Ava shook the bucket. The sheep feed it held rattled loudly against the sides.

'Come on, girls,' she said, trying to imitate Tom. Her voice sounded small, swallowed up by the trees. Ava cleared her throat and tried again.

'Come on!' she yelled. 'Come on!'

She continued to shake the bucket, worried the sheep feed might fly out.

Ava squinted into the woods. Dark shapes were moving between the trunks. There was a flash of black and white. The shapes were moving fast – the sheep were coming!

'Come on!'

She continued to call them and shake the bucket. The sheep emerged from the trees, coming towards her. Satisfied they were heading in the right direction, she jogged to the side of the gate, getting out of the way. As the sheep flowed into

the field, Tom came into sight, waving his arms to push them forward, heading off any stragglers. Jet darted gracefully behind them, funnelling the sheep through the opening.

'Gate!' yelled Tom.

Ava untied the gate from the fence and swung it shut as Tom and Jet came through. Tom took the bucket from Ava and tipped the feed into small piles on the grass. The sheep made a beeline for their reward.

'That was brilliant!' exclaimed Ava.

Tom smiled at her for a moment before apparently realizing what he'd done.

'Why are these sheep down here on their own?' Ava asked.

'They're too young to have lambs yet. They will next year though, so we keep them in a small flock together until then.'

Ava nodded. Even though she had been longing for home in the last couple of days, she was struck by a jolt of sadness. Ava would miss things like this, and she knew she wouldn't have time to learn everything about the farm.

Jet padded across the grass to Ava, stopping to sit next to her feet. He looked up at her with bright eyes, panting happily. Ava stooped to stroke him behind his ears.

'Good boy, Jet. You're a clever sheepdog,' whispered Ava.

Jet licked the side of Ava's face.

'Aw, Jet!' Ava laughed.

'Come on,' ordered Tom.

They walked along the line of fence that edged the woodland.

'We're looking for bits in the wire that are broken. Any big sections will have to be done with Mum and Dad, but we can do little fixes ourselves.'

Ava wasn't exactly sure what she was looking for, but she kept her eyes peeled for anything remotely out of place.

They walked in silence, both sets of eyes glued to the silvery wire designed to keep the sheep safe and secure. The morning clouds had cleared and the warm spring sun beat down on them, making Ava wish she'd brought her water bottle. She spotted a section of wire that didn't look quite right.

'There!' she said, pointing to a small, loose bit of wire.

Tom knelt to inspect it, pulling at the fence.

'That's not going to cause a problem, so we'll leave it.'

Ava felt a little deflated. She thought she'd found something that needed fixing.

'Here,' said Tom, pointing to a section a few metres along. 'This bit needs doing.' He pushed the wire and a gap appeared. 'A sheep could push through and get their head stuck.'

'Can we do this bit ourselves?' asked Ava.

Tom nodded. 'I think so.'

He opened up his rucksack. Ava could see a roll of thin wire, metal clippers and a bag of cable ties inside.

'It doesn't have to look pretty; it just has to do the job,' he said with a small smile. 'Here, hold this.'

Ava held the fence together as Tom bent the loose

bits of wire to pull the gap closed before securing it with more wire. Once he'd finished, they continued along the fence-line, stopping every so often to make minor repairs. They worked in silence, Tom avoiding Ava's attempts at conversation. He definitely hadn't forgiven her yet.

# Chapter Sixteen

# FENCES AND FRIENDS

The sun was high overhead, radiating its gentle warmth that encouraged the springtime awakening of the flora and fauna around them. They'd been working for a couple of hours and had now reached the part of the farm where the fields and woodland met the narrow country road that wove its way through the bottom of the valley. Ava hadn't seen a single vehicle pass by in the fifteen minutes they'd been there.

Jet was laid out on the grass, his keen eyes fixed on the sheep. It was amazing how he was ready to spring into action if needed. Tom was wrangling a tricky repair on his own, so Ava leaned against a metal gate and closed her eyes, listening to the sounds around her. There was a chorus of birdsong – high musical notes, shrill cackling sounds and intermittent screeches from high above. Ava wished she knew what birds they were. They mainly had pigeons in the garden at home, with the occasional robin that hopped across the patio.

'Do you know what the birds are by the sound they make?' she asked Tom curiously.

'What?'

'You know, can you tell which birds are singing?'

Tom frowned at her.

'What's that got to do with repairing the fence?'

'Nothing.' Ava shrugged. 'I'm just interested.' She looked at her cousin. 'If you don't know, that's fine.'

'Blackbird, robin and a red kite somewhere way up there,' he said with a sigh. 'Now can we get on with this? I'm supposed to be meeting my friends.'

Ava blinked in surprise. She couldn't help feeling impressed, and she made a mental note to learn about the most common birds – what they looked and sounded like. Tom went back to mending the wire.

'Cutters,' said Tom.

Ava reached into the rucksack. As she pulled the cutters free to hand them to Tom, the cable ties fell out, landing on the other side of the gate. She peered over the metal gate to grab them.

Ava frowned. A large patch of grass had been flattened, as if someone had walked up and down it several times. Ava felt uneasy as she noticed a set of tyre tracks in the gateway too.

'Tom. Look at this.'

'Mmmm.'

'Tom. I need to show you something.'

'Hang on . . . Nearly done . . .'

Tom stood to face her.

'This is weird, isn't it?' Ava nodded towards the gateway.

Tom looked for a moment before shrugging.

'The tyre marks and trampled grass,' said Ava, pointing to them.

Jet began sniffing the flattened grass.

'So?' said Tom.

'So, don't you think that's odd?'

Tom laughed. 'No.'

'But why are the tyre marks there?' asked Ava.

'Someone probably got lost and pulled in. Happens a lot round here. There aren't many places to stop on this tiny road.'

Ava shook her head. 'But what about the trampled grass?'

'They probably got out and stretched their legs.

Maybe they had a wee against the gatepost.'

'Eugh,' said Ava in disgust.

'What? I do it all the time.'

'Yuck, Tom!'

Tom smirked at her.

'The gate's locked anyway,' he said. 'Look.'

A chunky silver chain was wrapped round the metal gate, securing it to the fence post with a substantial lock.

But something didn't feel right to Ava – she remembered with a jolt that she hadn't told anyone about the man in the woods.

'I saw someone in the woods the other day.'

Tom hesitated.

'Where?'

'The other side of the farm. At the bottom of the hill fields where I found Hope.'

'What did they look like?'

'I'm not sure – I couldn't really see him properly.'

Tom put his hands on his hips and stared at her.

'Are you making this up?'

'No!' cried Ava.

'You can't even give me a description of this *person*.'

'They were wearing a hoodie—' Ava began.

'Of course they were,' said Tom, cutting her off.

'I'm telling the truth!'

'I don't believe you, Ava.'

'Why not?' she snapped.

'Everything's always about you. You're making it up to be the centre of attention again.'

'No, I'm not. I—'

'You think you're so much better than everyone else. But you're not, Ava.'

'Tom, I—'

A whistle stopped Ava mid-sentence. Tom looked along the lane and his stony face morphed into a large grin.

'Oi. Oi!' he called out, leaping up to perch on the gate.

Ava leaned forward to get a better view. A huddle of bikes screeched to a halt in the gateway. Four faces stared back at her. A boy on a muddy blue mountain bike looked at Tom.

'Who's your friend?'

Tom glanced at Ava.

'She's not my friend,' said Tom. 'She's my cousin.'

Ava felt like she was being scrutinized from top to toe. Her cheeks began to burn. She wished she was more confident in front of new people. A tall, dark-haired girl with light brown skin got off her glittery purple bike and made her way over, giving Tom a cold stare as she passed.

'If Tom isn't going to introduce us, then I will. I'm Jasmine.'

She smiled warmly at Ava.

'This is Jack,' said Jasmine, pointing to the blond boy that had asked Tom if she was his friend. 'And that's Rav and Bella.'

A mousy-haired girl with freckles and a smaller boy wearing glasses gave her a wave. Rav leaned over the gate and began ruffling Jet's ears.

They stood in silence for a moment before Jasmine turned to face Ava's cousin.

'Tom?'

Tom blinked at her.

'Oh, yeah. This is my cousin, Ava.'

Ava smiled nervously at them and was surprised

to find them all smiling back.

'She's staying with us for a bit,' muttered Tom.

'Well, it's lovely to meet you, Ava,' said Jasmine kindly.

'Are you coming then, Tom?' asked Jack impatiently.

'Yeah,' he said. 'I think we're just about done. Right, Ava?'

Ava knew they hadn't finished the fence but said nothing.

'You can come with us if you like, Ava?' said Jasmine warmly.

'Oh,' said Ava, surprised. 'Thank—'

'She can't,' Tom interrupted. 'Has stuff to do up at the farm, don't you, Ava?'

'Well, I . . .' Ava's words failed. It was clear Tom didn't want her to go with them.

'You're welcome to tag along with us, Ava,' Jasmine said softly.

Ava really wanted to join them – Jasmine

seemed so nice – but she didn't want to annoy her cousin.

'She wouldn't want to, Jas,' said Tom. 'She doesn't like the same stuff we do – she's from the city.'

Tom hopped onto the back of Jack's bike.

'See you later, Ava!' called Tom, as Jack started to pedal away. 'Watch out for "people" in the woods! Come on, Jet!'

Jet squeezed under the gate and ran alongside the bike. Rav and Bella set off after them as Jasmine got on her bike.

'Maybe see you another time?' said Jasmine.

Ava nodded quickly.

Jasmine disappeared round the bend of the narrow road and Ava slumped on the grass, head in her hands. Tom had her all wrong. How would he know what she liked to do? He'd barely asked her anything since she'd arrived. She breathed deeply, trying to relax.

Ava watched the sheep in the field for a while, losing herself in the playful antics of the flock. Lambs were skipping around together, but they didn't dare stray too far from the watchful eyes of their mothers. Ava sighed and resigned herself to heading back to the farmhouse – she was on her own again.

# Chapter Seventeen

# ALONE IN THE WOODS

Ava replayed her conversation with Tom in her head as she walked back to the farm through the woods. He'd been quick to dismiss Ava's uneasy feeling about the tyre tracks, but she reassured herself that there was a hefty chain securing the gate. Tom had accused her of making up the man in the woods, but she had seen him *and* she'd seen that light bobbing along the track the other night. Ava groaned. She'd forgotten to tell Tom about the light! Although he probably wasn't going to believe her about that either. She would have to tell Aunt Kitty and Uncle John herself. Surely they'd take her seriously?

A twig snapped somewhere in the woodland, making her jump and lose her train of thought.

'Come on, Ava,' she told herself. 'Don't let your imagination get the better of you.'

She put her head down and paced through the trees. She could have walked back to the farmhouse through the fields, but going through the woods was much quicker. A squirrel darted in front of her and Ava stopped. The squirrel stopped too. It twitched its grey bushy tail, its dark beady eyes fixed on her. It grabbed something from the floor, wary eyes still on Ava. The squirrel sat down, holding a small nut in its paws. It made a funny little chuntering sound before speeding off into the trees with its prize.

Ava looked around her – leaves sprang out of tree

branches everywhere, a sea of every shade of green. Somewhere through the trees, a flash of colour caught Ava's eye. She carefully picked her way over fallen branches and clumps of tufty grass until the trees thinned a little. Ava gasped. Dappled sunlight filtered through the spring canopy, illuminating a sea of beautiful violet–blue flowers on the woodland floor.

'Bluebells,' Ava whispered.

She remembered going on a 'bluebell walk' in the country with her parents a few years ago. They hadn't stayed long as the heavens had opened – Ava had been soaked to the bone, but she'd never forgotten the trail of beautiful bluebells they'd marched through. This, though, was something else entirely. The smell was incredible and she'd never seen this many bluebells in one place. Ava marvelled at the sight and decided bluebell was her new favourite colour.

*Crack. Crack.*

Ava spun round and scanned the woodland, searching for the source of the noise. She suddenly had an overwhelming feeling that she wasn't alone.

*Crack.*

Ava's heart raced as she heard another branch break and someone groan. Voices drifted towards her and she could hear them getting closer. Ava flattened herself against the nearest tree trunk, hoping the ancient oak would hide her. Maybe she was overreacting and it was Tom and his friends coming back. But it didn't sound like them. The voices sounded older.

Ava didn't know what to do. What if it was the figure in the hoodie again? She had a bad feeling about him, whoever he was. Besides there were *voices*, which meant there were *people*. If they were up to no good, there wasn't much she could do by herself.

A dog barked. It didn't sound like Jet. Ava could feel panic rising steadily inside her. A man's voice shouted as the dog barked again. Ava was no expert, but the dog sounded *big*.

The sounds were getting closer. Ava tried to clear her head, to work out the fastest route back to the farmhouse. The woods weren't familiar to her yet, so her escape route would have to be a best guess.

All at once, the voices were closing in on her.

Ava knew the time to make a run for it was now or never. As her welly hit the ground, a small branch snapped crisply underneath it. The sound reverberated round the woods, ricocheting off the tree trunks. The voices stopped. Ava could swear her heart stopped too. The silence was ominous and she felt the warning of danger prickle up her spine.

'Run,' she whispered to herself.

Ava stumbled forward, her wellies slipping on the woodland floor. She dashed ahead wildly, not daring to look back to see if she was being followed. Every nerve in her body was screaming at her to run faster.

She saw the low-hanging branch a little too late. Wisps of wood whipped at her face as she attempted to duck, stinging her cheek where they made contact. Ava pushed through the pain and continued to run, desperately hoping she was heading in the right direction. She clumsily navigated the uneven ground as she battled to stay upright.

Ava's heart lifted as she saw that the trees were thinning and the way ahead was getting lighter – she could just about see the sheep fields beyond the woods. She continued to run towards the safety of the farmhouse.

As she reached the edge of the woods, the sunlight hit her face and she was momentarily blinded. She shielded her eyes and ran straight into something. Ava flew backwards, landing hard on the floor. A shadow loomed over her.

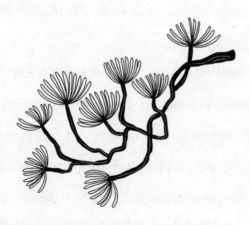

# Chapter Eighteen

# SOMETHING ISN'T RIGHT . . .

Ava squeezed her eyes shut. *Please don't hurt me,* she thought.

Ava heard the movement of people. She took a deep breath, willing herself to be brave.

'Watch it, idiot!'

Ava frowned. She opened one eye and looked up.

'Tom,' she breathed, relief rushing through her.

She squinted and saw the rest of Tom's friends looking down at her.

'Are you all right?' asked Jasmine, reaching out a hand.

Ava took it and Jasmine pulled her to her feet.

'What happened to your face?'

Jasmine's eyes were full of concern, but Ava didn't know what she meant. Then she remembered. Her cheek burned where she hadn't managed to duck the branch in time. Ava touched it tentatively, wincing as it stung. Her fingers felt sticky with what she could now see was blood.

'You should get that cleaned up,' said Jasmine softly.

She swiftly pulled her dark wavy hair out of its ponytail and held her scrunchie out.

'It's the best I can do, I'm afraid.' Jasmine shrugged.

Ava stared in confusion at the scrunchie.

'Here,' Jasmine said, stepping forward and

pressing the scrunchie onto the cut. 'It'll help stop the bleeding.'

'Thank you,' said Ava.

'What were you doing in there anyway?' asked Tom.

Ava glared at him. 'Running away!'

Tom's eyes widened. 'What?'

'There were people in the woods . . . with a dog.'

'What were they doing?' asked Rav, peering into the woods behind her.

'I don't know. I heard them . . . then I ran,' said Ava.

Tom frowned at Ava.

'So, let me get this right. You heard some people in the woods, with a dog.'

'Yes,' said Ava.

'But you didn't actually see them?'

Tom and his friends exchanged bemused glances.

'But they shouldn't be in there, Tom! It's private property, isn't it?'

Tom snorted. 'Just because people aren't supposed to be somewhere, doesn't mean they don't go.'

'It could've just been a family walking their dog,' suggested Bella with a reassuring smile.

'Or rabbiters,' said Jack with a tut. 'There's always someone in our woods trying to catch a rabbit or shoot a pheasant or summat.'

'Why do you always assume the worst in people, Ava?' Tom folded his arms.

'I don't!' shouted Ava, anger rising inside her. 'It's not just that – there's the other things too. I—'

Tom held his hand up. 'I don't have time for this. I only came back to grab my bike.'

'But, Tom, you've got to listen . . .'

'I don't *have* to do anything, Ava.' Tom took a step towards her. 'I want to hang out with my friends!'

Tom spun round and stomped away. Jack, Rav

and Bella followed him, but Jasmine hesitated.

'He's not normally this grumpy,' said Jasmine with a grimace. 'But if you're really worried about the people in the woods, then maybe you should try and talk to him again. And if he won't listen, then you should tell your aunt and uncle, no matter what he thinks.'

Ava glanced back towards the woods; she couldn't shake the feeling that something wasn't right.

'Tom, wait!'

Ava walked towards her cousin with Jasmine by her side.

'I don't want to hear any more, Ava. I want to go and have fun!'

Ava fixed him with the most intense stare she could muster.

'It doesn't matter what's happened between us or what you think of me, Tom. All I know is that something isn't right. The people in the woods just now, the weird grass at the gate, the hooded man! I saw a strange light outside the farmhouse the other night too! We need to tell your mum and dad about this.'

Tom's face faltered.

'Please, Tom, trust me on this.'

Tom's eyes widened. 'Trust you?' He shook his head. 'How can I trust you after . . . Whatever. If it makes you happy, *I'll* talk to Mum and Dad later and see what they think.'

With that, Tom marched off across the field towards the farmhouse, Jet by his side and flanked by his friends. Ava felt Jasmine's hand squeeze her shoulder as she followed them.

Despite Tom not taking her seriously, Ava felt a wave of relief. At least if he told Uncle John and Aunt Kitty about it all, maybe she wouldn't have to worry.

Her mum and dad flashed into her mind. They'd

believe her – she knew they would. But they were halfway round the world. Ava thought about calling them, but she knew they'd be busy and she didn't want to be a nuisance.

Ava glanced over her shoulder towards the woods and shivered. But the gentle spring sun wrapped round her, lifting her spirits just enough to shake her out of her worry.

Back at the farmhouse, Uncle John's green tractor was parked in the middle of the yard, but there was no sign of him. Ava navigated round a newly delivered stack of sheep feed and headed straight for Hope's barn – she needed to see her.

At the sight of Ava, Hope bounced towards her. Ava rubbed Hope's back and felt the lamb lean into her. It was such a small movement, but it showed Ava that Hope really trusted her.

Ava slid down the whitewashed wall to sit beside Hope. The lamb nestled against her, before resting her chin on Ava's thigh and falling asleep. This was just what Ava wanted right now. She felt completely content. It was nice to be needed by something – looking after Hope was the best thing she'd ever done. Ava leaned her head back against the wall, suddenly exhausted. She could stay like this for ever, just her and Hope, together.

# Chapter Nineteen

# BACK TO THE BARN

The door to the barn creaked open, startling Ava. It was gloomier than she remembered, and the crick in her neck brought the realization that she must have fallen asleep.

'You okay, Ava?' asked Uncle John from the doorway, a sack of sheep feed over his shoulder.

'Think so,' she croaked in reply, rubbing her neck and noticing her bum had gone numb. 'What time is it?'

'Just gone four,' said her uncle.

'What?' said Ava, trying to stand despite the pins and needles in her legs. She'd been asleep for a couple of hours.

'Your aunt needs you in the chicken barn for a bit,' said Uncle John.

Ava's stomach plummeted.

'But . . .'

'No buts, Ava. She'll see you in there when you've said goodbye to Hope. Don't be long.'

With that, her uncle disappeared, his heavy footsteps trailing away towards the storage barn. Ava felt the prickle of sweat on her back. She hadn't ventured to the chicken barn since that awful morning.

'I guess I've got to face it sometime,' she said to Hope.

*Baa.*

Ava stepped out into the courtyard. Tom's green

mountain bike was leaning against the wall, and she wondered if he'd told his mum and dad about the odd things she'd seen around the farm yet. She had hoped he'd still be out with his friends so she wouldn't have to face him *and* the chicken barn at the same time.

Ava hesitated by the door. The last time she'd been inside it, she'd decided she never wanted to set foot in there again. She pushed thoughts of the fox attack out of her mind as she reached for the door latch.

Neither Aunt Kitty nor Tom were anywhere to be seen. In fact, there wasn't much in there at all any more and the barn had been cleaned up completely. Ava's shoulders sagged as she realized what was missing: the comforting chatter of chickens.

Ava walked past the first empty chicken pen, her steps faltering. She hurried on, stopping outside the next one, where the few remaining chickens were

shut safely inside. The windows to the barn were open so a steady flow of fresh spring air swirled round the barn. Ava saw Tom perched on a bale of straw, holding a small brown chicken in his arms. He hadn't noticed Ava, and she didn't want to disturb him, so she hovered quietly.

Ava watched Tom cradle the tiny chicken that she could now see was his beloved Serama cockerel.

Complicated emotions swirled in her as she watched Tom stroke Loki. She felt relieved Tom still had Loki, but she remembered Tom's other favourite chicken, HB, would never be coming back.

'Ah, there you are.'

Aunt Kitty entered the barn, holding something in her hands, before setting it down on a table at the back.

'Help me set this up, love,' she said.

Ava glanced at Tom, who had put Loki on the floor.

'Here, put this in the socket.'

Aunt Kitty handed her a plug. Its wire was attached to some sort of box with a transparent lid.

'What is it?' asked Ava, plugging it in.

Aunt Kitty smiled.

'You're going to love this,' she replied.

Ava inspected the distinctly uninteresting plastic contraption on the table and wasn't so sure.

'Tom?' called Aunt Kitty. 'Have you got the eggs?'

Tom walked over, carefully cradling something in the bottom of his jumper.

'Is it an incubator?' Ava asked, unable to keep the excitement from her voice.

'*Duh . . .*' said Tom.

Aunt Kitty's face tightened.

'I'm going to leave you two to set this up,' she said quickly.

'But—' protested Tom.

'No buts, Thomas. And I don't want either of you coming back in until you've sorted out this ridiculous feud you're having.'

'Well, she should try and be more careful, shouldn't she?' muttered Tom.

'I've already said sorry about the fox, Tom!'

'And you're not so innocent yourself, young man,' said Aunt Kitty coolly.

Ava's mouth dropped open.

'How dare you tell Ava no one wanted her here! Forget the fact it was a total lie, it was a very unkind and hurtful thing to say!'

The colour drained from Tom's face.

Ava shifted uncomfortably on her feet as she looked at the floor.

'And don't you blame Ava either. She didn't want to tell me about it, but she was so upset that I *made* her tell me. She stuck up for you too, Tom, which I'm not sure you really deserved. I don't care how hurt you were about what happened to the chickens. Ava's family, and you don't lie to your family!'

Aunt Kitty was shaking now and her voice was strained. Ava had never seen her this upset.

'Now. I want the pair of you to sort out your differences. Ava's not here for much longer and I don't want you to part on bad terms. Family should be there for each other no matter what.'

Aunt Kitty brushed some imaginary dirt from her jacket as she composed herself.

'I'll see you both inside for tea when you've set up the incubator and formed a truce. Do I make myself clear?'

'Yes, Aunt Kitty.'

'Yes, Mum.'

Tom and Ava stood in an awkward silence in the chicken barn.

'I can't believe you grassed me up,' muttered Tom.

'You heard her – she forced it out of me!'

Tom sighed. 'Maybe we should just try and stay out of each other's way.'

'I don't like it when we fight, Tom. It's awful.'

Ava saw Tom's face soften.

'I guess I shouldn't have said no one wanted you

here. Mum and Dad were really looking forward to it.'

'And what about you?'

Tom briefly made eye contact with her, then shrugged.

'I didn't want to have to babysit you. I love the holidays. I get to spend all day on the farm. I didn't want *anyone* to spoil that. Especially . . .'

'Especially what?'

'Especially someone who doesn't know what they're doing and isn't even interested.'

Ava was about to shout at Tom that he had it all wrong but stopped herself. She heard her mum's advice in her head: *Always try to look at a situation from the other side before making your mind up.* And she *could* understand Tom's point of view – she'd never shown any interest in the farm before. How was Tom to know she was beginning to love it?

'Look, Tom, let's just try and get along for the

last few days that I'm here. Your mum's right – I'll be gone soon and your life can go back to the way it was. Neither of us wants to be miserable until my parents get back.'

Tom nodded slowly. He spat on his right hand and held it out to her. Ava's face must have betrayed her horror, as Tom burst out laughing. Ava's jaw dropped – she'd never heard her cousin laugh like that before. Tom wiped his hand on his tracksuit bottoms before holding it out again to Ava. This time she took it, shaking on their delicate truce.

'Oh, the eggs!' cried Ava.

A couple of them were dangerously close to falling out of Tom's jumper. Tom quickly readjusted it to keep them safe.

'Okay. See that jug of water over there?' said Tom. 'Grab it and pour some into the bottom of the incubator.'

Ava carefully did as she was instructed.

'That's enough,' said Tom. 'Right, see that black tray-like thing with holes in?'

'Yep,' said Ava, picking it up.

'Put that in the bottom so it sits just above the water.'

'Okay, done. What's this bit for?' asked Ava, holding up a piece that reminded her of a noughts-and-crosses grid.

'That goes in next. It holds the eggs in place so they can't roll about everywhere. We'll take it out for the last few days so the chicks have room to hatch.'

Ava put it into the incubator and then looked expectantly at Tom.

'Switch it on then,' said Tom impatiently.

'Oh. Right,' said Ava.

She flicked the switch and the incubator began to hum softly.

'Normally, we would have set this up earlier so

it could reach the perfect conditions inside, but we don't have time for that.'

'What do you mean?' asked Ava.

Tom flicked his head back towards the chicken run. 'One of the girls has stopped sitting on her eggs, so we're putting them in the incubator to see if we can get them to hatch. Normally, she doesn't leave her eggs for anything, but something's put her off. Could be she was spooked by the fo— I mean she's probably unsettled.'

Ava was grateful Tom changed the end of his sentence.

'Well, we need to do what we can to save them then, don't we?' said Ava, trying to sound upbeat.

Ava picked up one of the eggs from Tom's makeshift jumper basket and put it in the incubator.

'Other way up,' said Tom. 'Pointy end down.'

'You mean there's a right way?' asked Ava, not sure if Tom was joking or not.

'Yep. It's the best way to incubate them. There's an air sac in the rounder end and that should be at the top.'

Tom didn't sound like he was pulling her leg.

'Quickly, Ava. We don't want them to get too cold, otherwise they'll never hatch!'

As swiftly as she dared, Ava transferred the eggs to the incubator tray. When the last one was in, Tom put the lid on and checked the settings.

'It's quite a science,' said Tom, adjusting one of the buttons. 'It has to be the right temperature and humidity.'

'But don't the chickens usually, you know, just sit on them? How scientific is that?' said Ava.

Tom laughed. 'Well, that's what we're trying to mimic, isn't it?'

'I guess so,' said Ava.

The incubator suddenly made an odd grinding sound.

'Oh no! Have I done something wrong?' asked Ava.

Tom laughed and shook his head.

'It's just turning the eggs.'

'Turning them?'

'You really don't know much about animals and farm stuff, do you, Ava?' said Tom, shaking his head. 'A hen turns the eggs every so often, so that's what the incubator does too. We'll shut the mechanism off soon so the chicks can get used to knowing which way is up. Then they can get themselves out whenever they're ready.'

'How long until they hatch?' asked Ava, bending down to look at the eggs.

Tom shrugged. 'It's usually twenty-one days. The hen's been sitting on them for a couple of weeks already, so it shouldn't be too long.'

Tom nudged Ava gently.

'Once they hatch, we can put more eggs in the

incubator. It'll be the best chance of getting as many chicks hatching as possible. We'll be able to do this again before you go.'

Ava smiled. 'I'd like that.'

# Chapter Twenty

# THE TRUCE

The following morning, Ava woke up face to face with Hope.

*Baa.* Hope's wet nose nuzzled into Ava's neck.

'Morning,' croaked Ava. She stretched, her back felt stiff from lying on the barn floor overnight.

*Baa.* Hope was persistent.

'Yes, I know – you want your breakfast,' said Ava with a yawn.

Despite the chilly morning and achiness, she was

going to miss this. With only a few days left on the farm, she was determined to make the most of spending time with Hope. She could sleep in a bed any time.

Ava fetched Hope her bottle, then went to check on the incubator in the chicken barn. She hadn't expected to see anything hatching this morning but couldn't resist taking a look before breakfast. The grid to hold the eggs had gone, and she felt a tingle of excitement that they might be close to hatching.

Uncle John had gone to a farm sale earlier that morning, so breakfast was with just Tom and Aunt Kitty. Tom hadn't exactly been *chatty*, but he'd given her a nod and said good morning. This, Ava could live with.

'What time will Uncle John be back?' asked Ava.

'Tonight,' said Aunt Kitty, draining the last mouthfuls of tea from her mug. 'And while he's away, there's a day of fun and frivolity for me. Farm accounts!'

'Fun?' asked Ava in surprise.

Aunt Kitty laughed and stood up.

'No, Ava, not fun,' she whispered. 'But they won't do themselves, and no one else round here will do them.'

'Oh,' said Ava.

'I'll leave you two to finish off outside. I'll be in the office if you need me, but I'd rather not be disturbed if possible!'

'No problem, Mum,' said Tom.

Aunt Kitty looked from Tom to Ava.

'Thanks for working out your differences. And just to show how happy you've made me, I'll make two puddings tonight.'

Ava and Tom grinned at each other.

'Sounds good to me!' said Ava.

Tom and Ava headed outside, where Ava gave

Jet a tummy rub, then prepared his breakfast. Tom fed Harris, sneaking him another carrot, and they checked on the lambing shed together. All was quiet, but Ava noticed a few more newborn lambs. Ava watched them drinking from their mothers and felt a bubble of happiness in her chest. The bubble deflated a little as she remembered she wouldn't be able to do this for much longer.

'Come on, Ava. Just the chickens left to do,' said Tom.

Ava jogged behind him as he left the lambing shed.

'What shall we do when we're done?' asked Ava.

Tom stopped and turned to look at her.

'You can do whatever you like,' he said with a frown.

'Oh.'

'I'm going to meet my mates, so you've got the rest of the day to yourself.'

Obviously, the truce between them was just that – a truce. Nothing more, nothing less. She felt silly for assuming they were going to hang out together. Ava trudged up to the chicken barn and finished feeding up with Tom in silence. He didn't seem to notice anything was wrong, and she didn't have the courage to ask him if she could tag along.

'All done!' said Tom with a grin. 'See you later.'

He ran past Ava, grabbing his mountain bike and helmet. Ava managed a weak smile and watched him ride off down the farm track. She sighed. She really didn't want to spend the day on her own again. Why hadn't she just asked Tom if she could go too? Right at this moment, she'd like nothing more than to hang out with Tom and his school friends.

# Chapter Twenty-one

# THE CHAIN

Ava was trying to keep herself busy. So far, she'd found Uncle John's binoculars and birdwatched, eaten the ham sandwiches Aunt Kitty had left out for lunch and managed to speak to her parents despite the time difference. It had been wonderful to hear their voices, but on this call she'd done most of the talking, rambling on about Hope and all the other animals.

It was now mid-afternoon, and Ava was walking

a complete circuit of the farm to while away the last couple of hours until teatime. She found herself in the hill field where she'd first picked up Hope and was overjoyed to see the abundance of lambs that had arrived since. They skipped and played together, racing each other along the fence-line.

A high-pitched squeak caught her attention and she snapped her head in its direction, seeing a tiny mouse scuttling through the grass into the base of the hedgerow. Just ahead of her, a rabbit hopped across the field. There was life everywhere.

The woods came into view up ahead and Ava's mood dropped. She gave the woodland a wide berth, cutting across the middle of the bottom hill field so she didn't get too close. She felt a prickle of fear across her neck – what if the hooded man came back? The thought of that made Ava wonder again whether Tom had spoken to his mum and dad about it all yet.

Ava climbed over the fence into the next field

and caught sight of Harris. He spotted her and began sauntering in her direction. When he finally reached Ava, he nuzzled into her, pushing his nose into her pockets.

'That's the only reason you come and say hello, isn't it, boy?' said Ava with a giggle. 'You're forever hopeful there'll be something tasty in my pocket!'

Ava stroked his coarse rusty-brown hair. He was a beautiful Shetland, despite his ancient years – Aunt Kitty said he must have been about twenty. He had a large patch of white on his back that was almost saddle shaped. As Ava stroked him, she wondered whether he'd somehow picked up on her feelings and was trying to lift her spirits. Whatever it was, Ava let the moment take her, enjoying their time together.

After a few minutes, Harris gently snorted and walked away. Ava decided she was going to come and see Harris every day until she left.

Determined to finish her lap of the farm before the light faded, Ava marched down towards the last couple of sheep fields. There didn't seem to be any pregnant ewes left in the fields; they all had lambs at their feet. She decided to check on her fence repairs from the day before. Ava scanned the fence, picking out the sections she and Tom had patched up.

'Not bad,' muttered Ava as she admired their handiwork.

She leaned over the gateway, looking up and down the road that ran alongside the farm.

It had rained overnight, and the tyre marks she'd seen before had been washed away. Ava frowned as her eyes fell on the gate chain. There was something different about it. Ava took hold of the metal links, and the heavy chain fell away in her hands! She picked it up, examining it closely. The hefty padlock was still locked, but it looked like the chain had been cut. There was nothing to keep the gate shut any more – anyone could open it!

What was going on? Ava's heart was racing.

She looked at the ends of the chain again. It wasn't an accident. Someone had cut it on purpose. But why would anyone do that? Uncle John or Aunt Kitty would have used the key for the padlock if they'd wanted to open it. Ava's sense of unease grew. She also realized that someone must have hung the chain back in place so it looked like it was still in one piece.

'I need to tell Aunt Kitty,' muttered Ava breathlessly.

She fumbled in her pocket for her phone. She groaned as she saw the black screen. It had run out of battery. Ava sighed, she kept forgetting to charge it.

Voices drifted towards her from along the road.

Trying to stay calm, she leaned over the gate for a better look. Her heart skipped as she saw who it was.

'Tom!' shouted Ava.

'What the . . .'

There was the noise of squealing bike brakes as Tom swerved in surprise. Ava watched in horror as his front wheel hit a pothole and he fell off. Four other bikes screeched to a stop behind him.

Gingerly, Tom picked himself up from the road, examining his elbow. His jumper had ripped, and Ava could see blood glistening from a nasty graze. He glared in Ava's direction.

'What are you playing at!' Tom shouted.

Ava blinked. 'I . . . I didn't mean to startle you . . .'

'Well, you did!' roared Tom.

Jasmine, Jack, Rav and Bella stood motionless astride their bikes behind him.

'Are you okay?' said Ava quietly, looking away from Tom's injured elbow.

'What do you think?' hissed Tom.

'I'm sorry, Tom. I didn't mean for you to fall off. I just heard you coming and . . .'

Tom picked up his bike, his face crimson with embarrassment.

'Please, Tom,' said Ava.

'Just leave it, Ava! Just when I start to think maybe you're okay, you go and do something stupid again! You could have really hurt me!'

Ava winced – Tom clearly thought his tumble was all her fault, but she hadn't meant to startle him. At any other time, she would have let him leave to save his pride, but she couldn't do that right now.

'But, Tom, I need to show you something.'

Tom was about to get on his bike, but his eyes fell on the chain in Ava's hands.

'What have you done to that?' he asked, his eyes dark.

'I just found it like this,' replied Ava.

Tom frowned, still looking at the severed chain.

'Tom, I'm telling the truth. I think it's connected to all the other things I've seen.'

'Oh, not this again!'

Tom got on his saddle.

'What did your mum and dad say when you told them about everything?' asked Ava.

Tom said nothing and adjusted the cycle helmet on his head.

Ava's heart sank as she realized.

'You didn't tell them, did you?'

Tom sighed and put his foot on the pedal.

'No, I didn't. I don't want to bother them with any of this. They're too busy with the farm to get caught up in your overactive imagination! They've got enough to think about.'

'But, Tom . . .'

Tom rode away, with his friends pedalling closely behind him. Ava looked at the chain in her hands.

She wasn't imagining it – something was very wrong. She knew her aunt and uncle were busy, but they needed to know, no matter what Tom thought. It was time to take matters into her own hands.

# Chapter Twenty-two

# TROUBLE

By the time Ava made it back to the farmhouse, daylight had faded and the first stars were appearing in the darkening sky. Ava was disappointed to see Uncle John's truck wasn't back yet. She decided she had to tell Aunt Kitty about everything that had been going on anyway.

Ava let herself in through the front door and the smell of something delicious greeted her. She kicked off her wellies, hung up her jacket and plugged her in phone to charge. She'd seen Tom's bike outside and wondered if he'd already told Aunt Kitty what had happened on the road. She was willing to bet he hadn't mentioned the chain or the other strange happenings though. Ava wished she'd done it herself already. She hesitated by the kitchen door, suddenly feeling nervous – why had she waited so long to tell them? Ava gingerly pushed the door open and saw Aunt Kitty taking a shepherd's pie out of the oven.

'Ah, there you are!' said Aunt Kitty brightly, clearly unaware of what had happened.

There was no sign of Tom.

'Sit down, love. Grab it while it's hot! Tom's just cleaning himself up. Your uncle's held up at the farm sale, so it's just us for now.'

Ava opened her mouth to tell Aunt Kitty everything. But before the words could come tumbling out, the kitchen door opened and Tom stood there with one sleeve rolled up, the deep wound on his elbow clearly visible. It looked bad. Ava bit her lip, knowing Aunt Kitty would see it any second.

'Tom!' screeched Aunt Kitty, depositing a bowl of mashed carrot and swede on the table. 'What on earth happened to you? Why didn't you say anything when you came in?'

Aunt Kitty was inspecting the wound closely while Tom said nothing. He just stared at Ava. Aunt Kitty looked up at him and frowned. She followed his gaze towards her. Ava slumped down in her seat, her cheeks burning under their stares.

'It was her fault,' muttered Tom.

Aunt Kitty's eyes widened, but she didn't say anything. She strode over to a cupboard and pulled out a first-aid box. She swiftly cleaned the gash on Tom's elbow. No one said a word while she worked. Ava stared at the shepherd's pie on the table, trying to work out how she could best explain the accident.

After a couple of minutes, Aunt Kitty finished dressing the wound. She washed and dried her hands, still without speaking, before turning to face them.

'Right. Now, I want to know exactly what happened.' Aunt Kitty's tone was firm.

'She—' Tom butted in.

Aunt Kitty held up her hand.

'From *each* of you. Tom, you can go first, as you obviously want to get it off your chest. Ava, you will not speak until he's finished. Then you can tell me your version.'

'She knocked me off my bike, Mum!'

Ava opened her mouth to object but thought better of it.

'And how exactly did she knock you off your bike?'

'I was riding along when she suddenly shouted at me out of nowhere! I was so shocked, there was no way I could have stayed on my bike. I could have been run over! I could have died, Mum!'

Ava wasn't surprised he was laying it on thick.

'You were on the road?' asked Aunt Kitty quietly.

The distress in Aunt Kitty's voice ignited the regret simmering inside Ava.

'Yeah. She did it on purpose! I could have broken my arm!'

Tom crossed his arms and narrowed his eyes at Ava.

*It can't hurt that much if you can fold your arms,* thought Ava.

'And what's your side of this, Ava?' asked Aunt Kitty.

Ava sighed.

'It was my fault Tom fell off his bike, but I didn't mean for it to happen!'

'Yeah. Just like the chickens,' muttered Tom.

Aunt Kitty gave him a withering stare.

'Go on, Ava,' she said.

'I heard Tom coming along the road and I called out to get his attention. I didn't mean to startle him so he fell off. I just wanted to show him the chain.'

Aunt Kitty's brow creased.

'The chain? What chain?'

'Just leave it, Ava!' Tom shook his head.

'That's enough, Thomas!'

'I was trying to show Tom the chain from the gate at the bottom field. The one that meets the road. Someone's cut it!'

'What?' said Aunt Kitty, looking from Tom to Ava and back again.

'I don't think it's been cut, Mum,' said Tom dismissively.

'It was cut, Tom! I'm not an idiot! Anyone could see it was!'

Tom snorted at her.

'Can I see it?' asked Aunt Kitty, her voice tight.

'She's just overreacting, Mum.'

'I'll decide whether she is or not, Tom,' said Aunt Kitty.

A glimmer of satisfaction fizzed inside Ava.

'Where's the chain?' asked Aunt Kitty.

Ava's shoulders sagged as she realized her mistake.

'I . . . er . . . I haven't got it. I left it on the gate.'

Tom snorted again.

'And she says she's not an idiot.'

'Stop!' Aunt Kitty yelled across the table, making them both jump. 'I've had enough of you two this week!'

Ava was startled by Aunt Kitty's explosion, and she could see by Tom's face he was too.

'But what about the chain?' asked Ava quietly.

'Seeing as the chain's down in the far field and it's dark now, I'll have to look at it in the morning. John will be back by then and we can go down together.'

'Sorry, Aunt Kitty,' Ava whispered.

'*Sorry, Aunt Kitty,*' mimicked Tom.

Aunt Kitty had a white-knuckle grip on the kitchen table.

'Both of you, plate up your tea and go straight to your rooms. We'll talk about this again in the morning.'

Aunt Kitty didn't wait for an answer. She turned away and disappeared out of the kitchen.

'Well done,' whispered Tom. 'She hardly ever gets that angry.'

'It's not my fault!' Ava hissed back, digging a spoon into the shepherd's pie.

'Yeah, it is!'

'Your mum's so cross now, I didn't get a chance to tell her about the man in the woods, the light in the middle of the night and the tyre tracks. I've got a really bad feeling about it all. What if something happens down at the gate?' said Ava.

'Like what?' said Tom.

Ava shrugged. 'I don't know . . . We could stake it out, make sure everything's okay.'

'We're not detectives, Ava. Besides, you heard Mum. It's too dark to do anything about it now.'

Ava turned away and headed towards the front door with her loaded plate and cutlery, yanking her phone from the charger as she passed.

'Where are you going?' asked Tom.

'To spend the night with Hope. The conversation's better.'

Ava couldn't help but smile as she stepped out of the front door. She knew Tom would stew on the fact she said she'd rather talk to a lamb than him. She thought he deserved it, just a little bit.

# Chapter Twenty-three

# A SLEEPLESS NIGHT

Ava's breath misted as it hit the cold air in the barn. The spring sun may be warm during the day, but the temperature plummeted at night.

Ava squinted at Hope, her black features hard to pick out in the near-darkness. There was just a sliver of moonlight through the small window tonight, and the only other source of light in the barn was from the heat-lamp. Hope's body was warm next to Ava's and she was snoring softly.

Ava carefully reached into her sleeping bag, trying to move quietly so she didn't wake Hope. She delved into her pocket and pulled out her phone. The artificial light stung her eyes, making her blink. Slowly, her eyes focused.

00:14

Ava hadn't been to sleep yet: thoughts of hooded men, big dogs and sabotaged gates swirled in her mind. It was impossible to drift off. Aunt Kitty had seemed concerned about the severed chain, and Ava wished she'd told her about everything else sooner. Maybe if she had, she'd be sleeping soundly now. Ava sighed and checked her phone again.

00:16

She couldn't shake the feeling of dread that nestled deep in the pit of her stomach. She'd already caused a devastating fox attack; she didn't want to be responsible for another disaster just because she hadn't had the courage to speak up. But Aunt Kitty hadn't given her a chance to mention anything other than the chain. Why hadn't she just blurted it out rather than being embarrassed that she'd left the chain behind? Ava couldn't shake the feeling that all these things weren't a coincidence.

There was no way she was getting any sleep tonight. She couldn't stand by and let something bad unfold. *She* had to do something, even if it was all by herself. It was time for a stakeout.

Ava gently pushed herself away from Hope and began to wriggle slowly out of the sleeping bag. Halfway out, Hope stirred. Ava's body went rigid, and she held her breath. The last thing she needed was Hope waking up.

Ava finally heard Hope's gentle rhythmic snores again. She finished easing herself out of the sleeping bag and stood up, silently slipping her feet into her green wellies. As she walked towards the barn door, the straw beneath her wellies crinkled, but the sound was soft enough not to wake the sleeping lamb. Ava reached for the door latch and prayed it would open silently, unlike the other latches and bolts on the farm. She smiled with relief as it opened without a whisper and she pulled the door towards her.

*Creeeaaakk.*

The door was stiff and rusty on its ancient hinges and Ava couldn't stop the sound. She held her breath, but she already knew it was too late. A rustling in the straw confirmed it.

*Baa.*

Hope unsteadily got to her feet, illuminated by the soft glow of the heat-lamp. Ava hesitated, trying to work out if she should quickly slip out of the barn or go back to settle the lamb.

*Baa.*

Hope stumbled towards Ava, bleating loudly.

*Baa. Baa.*

Ava crouched down and tickled Hope's chin.

'It's the middle of the night,' she whispered softly. 'Go back to sleep.'

Ava turned to leave again, pulling the door open wider.

*Baa. Baaa. Baaaaa.*

'Shhh. You'll wake the whole farm, Hope!'

She reached down and picked up the lamb, who instantly quietened in her arms.

'Please, Hope. I've just got to do something important. I'll be back soon.'

She placed Hope down on the straw and tried to leave again.

*Baa. Baaaaa.*

'Hope, no! I'm in enough trouble already without you adding to it!'

An idea flashed through Ava's mind. She wasn't sure if it was the best one she'd ever had, but she couldn't think of an alternative. Ava picked up Hope again, who fell silent.

'Look, Hope,' whispered Ava as she stroked the lamb's head. 'If you promise to be quiet, I'll take you down to the field gate and you can stake it out with me. We'll both have some company, and you get a midnight adventure. What do you think?'

*Baa.*

'Deal,' whispered Ava.

Ava slipped out of the barn with Hope clasped tightly across her chest. The lamb was growing fast and was getting heavy now. Ava didn't know if she'd be able to carry her all night. She smiled as an idea formed.

'We need to make a quick stop at the house,' she whispered to Hope.

Ava approached the farmhouse and spotted Uncle John's truck parked out the front. Somehow, it made Ava feel safer and more confident about what she was doing with the whole family there.

She quietly opened the door to the house,

knowing it would be unlocked – Aunt Kitty always left it open when she slept in the barn. Ava crept into the utility room, where she found what she was looking for. She grabbed Tom's rucksack, relieved to see it was empty. Ava cast her eyes around for a torch, but she couldn't see one. She tiptoed back to the front door, taking Tom's camouflage jacket as she left. Ava's feet crunched on the farm track and she caught her breath – would they hear it in the house? There was no movement behind the drawn curtains upstairs, so she carried on, before stopping further down the track.

'Okay, Hope, this might feel a bit strange at first, but you're going to like it, I know you will.'

Ava set Hope down on the ground and opened up the rucksack. Before Hope could protest, Ava put her inside the bag, making sure her head poked out of the top. She zipped up the sides so Hope couldn't fall out.

Ava hoisted the rucksack onto her front like a makeshift baby carrier. She stroked Hope's head, whispering to her softly. She must look totally ridiculous, but at least there was no one around to see her. Hope was quiet and content, and Ava was glad she wasn't alone. Tom may not have wanted to come with her, but at least she had Hope for company.

# Chapter Twenty-four

# THE STAKEOUT

Ava reached the field by the road, navigating her way in the small amount of moonlight that seeped through the cloud cover. The field was quiet, and Ava could just make out the shapes of the sheep.

The farm felt completely different at night. It seemed wilder and almost magical, like anything could happen. An owl hooted from somewhere in the woodland, and Ava wondered if it could see her, its eyes accustomed to the dark of night. At some point on the walk down, Hope had fallen asleep in Tom's rucksack. She didn't stir as Ava climbed over the gate and into the field.

The clouds shifted, bathing the field with moonlight and bringing the far gate into view. Ava walked towards it, ignoring the woods to her right, which were even more unsettling in the dark.

The gate was shut and the chain hung loosely, just how Ava had left it.

'So far, so good,' Ava whispered.

Ava looked around for a good place to hide and keep watch. Now she was here, she was determined to stay for the whole night.

She spotted a bush nearby that looked like the perfect hiding spot. It had grown through from the woodland and made a hole in the fence where its weight had broken the wire. Ava crouched behind it and peered round the leaves; her view was perfect. She waited, staring at the metal gate, unsure about what she was actually waiting *for*.

Night-time sounds from the woodland next to her – rustles, cracks and squeaks – put her on edge, but thankfully there was no sign of people or big dogs. Ava felt the comforting shape of her phone inside her coat pocket. If anything happened, or she saw anyone at all, she would call the farmhouse immediately.

Ava's legs began to cramp as she knelt. She moved herself so she was laid out, propped up on an elbow and legs stretched out, but still hidden from view. The dampness from the grass was beginning to soak through her trousers.

'I didn't think this through properly, did I?' Ava whispered to a sleeping Hope.

Even though she had Hope with her, she strangely wished Tom was there too. Ava felt a twinge of guilt: she'd be in so much trouble if her aunt and uncle knew what she was doing. Her mum and dad would be angry too, but they also wouldn't believe she'd plucked up the courage to do something like this.

Ava fixed her eyes on the gate. She would be ready and waiting for whatever or whoever was coming.

Ava jerked awake. She tried to shake away the fuzziness of sleep as a metallic clang rang in her ears. Ava blinked, registering low, muffled voices coming from somewhere nearby. She lifted her head and brushed the damp grass from her cheek, finally realizing that she must have dozed off. Hope stirred in the rucksack and Ava pulled herself up to a sitting position. She heard hushed voices and the sound of a gate creaking open. Ava peeked round the side of the bush. Figures were moving in the gateway, each with a low-lit head torch. Panic washed over Ava and she pulled back behind the bush to hide.

'What are they doing?' she whispered under her breath.

*Baa.*

'Shh, Hope,' she whispered, stroking the lamb.

Ava spied round the bush again, watching the figures move. The gate was wide open with a vehicle parked between the posts. Two of the figures strode into the field while a third stayed by the vehicle, keeping watch. To Ava's horror, this figure suddenly headed her way. She ducked further behind the bush and held her breath, willing Hope to stay silent.

The lookout passed by before doubling back — they had only been a few centimetres away from her! She let out her breath and peeked round the bush again. Sheep and lambs began to bleat in the field as the other two people moved round behind them. Ava turned her head towards the lookout, who was back at the gate. Their head torch lit up a

large metal dome, and Ava realized with a jolt that it was a sheep trailer. She watched in horror as the flock was herded towards it.

Ava fumbled in her coat pocket, her hand grasping her phone. She yanked it out and touched the screen. Nothing happened. Ava jabbed at it again, but the screen remained dark. Ava's stomach lurched – it had run out of charge again! She heard the clatter of feet running into the trailer.

She had to do something. But what *could* she do?

An idea sprang into her mind, but she wasn't sure it was a good one. Ava braced herself and stepped out from behind the bush.

'Hey!' she yelled.

Three head torches spun in her direction. They lit her up, making her feel exposed and vulnerable. She couldn't see anything of the people wearing them. Ava waved the dead phone at them.

'I've already called the police. They're on their way.'

A heavy silence followed as the figures looked at each other.

'I've called my uncle too. He'll be down in a minute, so you might want to leave.'

Ava held her breath, hoping they'd believe her lie. Then she heard a car door opening.

*Woof.*

Ava panicked. It sounded like the big dog from the woods. Her eyes widened in terror as she registered a large shape bounding towards her. She turned and ran – shouts and metallic bangs ringing out behind her.

Ava tripped on a divot and plummeted to the ground. The dog barked again and Ava scrambled to her feet. She could just about see the gate back to the farm track and ran as fast as she could towards it. Ava leaped over the gate and landed heavily on the other side. Pain shot through her ankle like a lightning bolt. She tried to ignore it and continued running towards the farmhouse. Her chest burned, and her ankle was agony, but she couldn't stop. She crashed through the front door and lifted the rucksack off her chest. She looked down with a sickening realization.

'Hope?' she whispered.

The rucksack was empty.

# Chapter Twenty-five

# MISSING SHEEP

Ava hobbled up the stairs in her wellies as fast as she could, vaguely thinking Aunt Kitty would go spare if she trod mud through the house. The door to her uncle and aunt's room swung open and Uncle John stood on the landing in his pyjamas.

'Ava?'

Ava's breaths were loud and mixed with sobs. Aunt Kitty appeared behind Uncle John, her face draining of colour as she saw Ava. She dashed forward, putting her arms round her.

'What's the matter?' she asked, her voice full of concern.

Ava tried to speak, but she just whimpered. Aunt Kitty squeezed her tighter.

'Try to calm down, sweetheart.'

Tom appeared from his bedroom door, rubbing his eyes.

'What's going on?' he said with a yawn. He caught sight of Ava and his eyes widened in shock.

'Help. I . . . need . . . help,' Ava managed to blurt out.

'What do you mean?' said Uncle John, stepping towards Ava.

'Someone's trying to steal the sheep in the bottom field!' she wailed.

'What?' said Aunt Kitty and Uncle John in unison.

'I've just come from there. They were putting them in a trailer.'

Uncle John and Aunt Kitty sprang into action. They raced downstairs to grab their coats and wellies. Ava and Tom followed.

'Truck keys,' shouted Uncle John.

Tom reacted quickly, grabbing the keys from the hook and throwing them to his dad. Tom grabbed his own wellies and made to go after his parents.

'Stay here,' ordered Uncle John.

'But . . .' protested Tom.

'Both of you,' he said.

'But Hope's out there,' sobbed Ava, trying to push past him. 'She was making so much noise and I didn't want to wake anyone. I took her with me to watch the gate. But I fell when the dog chased me and . . .'

'Dog?' asked Uncle John, his face pale.

'They set the dog on me, and I ran. But I tripped! I lost Hope! They might've taken her!'

Uncle John stepped forward and hugged Ava tightly.

'We'll find her, Ava.'

'But I can help!'

'No,' said her uncle firmly. 'I'd never forgive myself if anything happened to you. We need you both to hold the fort here.'

Uncle John and Aunt Kitty sprinted to the truck. The engine roared into life, and Ava watched helplessly as they sped away. Ava's shoulders slumped as she stood in the doorway, tears streaming down her face.

'Please find Hope,' she muttered.

'They will, Ava,' said Tom quietly.

Ava spun round to face her cousin.

'And what if they don't? If you'd believed me in the first place, maybe she wouldn't be missing!'

Ava pushed past him into the kitchen. Tom lingered in the doorway, watching her limp up and down in front of the range, her wellies slapping loudly on the tiled floor. He went over to the kettle and flicked it on.

'Tea?' he said brightly.

Ava glared at him.

'It's not the answer to everything!' she cried. 'How can you drink tea at a time like this!'

Tom's face flushed as he flicked the kettle off. He leaned against the worktop and stared at his feet. Ava collapsed onto a chair at the table. Her ankle throbbed painfully, so she bent down and eased off her welly and sock. A dark, angry bruise was already forming, and Tom noticed it right away.

Swiftly, he took out a bag of peas from the freezer and covered them with a tea towel, before pulling out the chair next to Ava and kneeling beside her.

'Put your foot on that,' he said, nodding to the chair.

Ava crossed her arms and looked away from him.

'Please, Ava. It looks painful.'

'Leave me alone.'

'Ava, let me help you. You might need to walk on it later to help Mum and Dad find Hope.'

Ava's eyes met Tom's. She reluctantly lifted her foot and rested it on the chair, wincing in agony as she moved. Tom placed the peas softly on Ava's swollen ankle. He was much gentler than she'd expected.

'You need to sit like that for a little while. Ice and elevation help.'

Ava said nothing. Tom went to sit opposite her.

'I'm sorry I didn't believe you,' he said quietly.

Ava raised her eyebrows. Tears pricked in her eyes and her throat felt thick.

'I know it doesn't change what's happened,' said Tom, 'but I am sorry. I can't bear the thought of the sheep being stolen or Hope being lost.'

They sat in silence again. The clock on the wall

ticked loudly and Ava's worry grew as she listened to the minutes go by without any news.

Suddenly the house phone rang, making them both jump. Tom leaped up to answer it.

'Okay . . . Right . . . What did the police say? Okay . . .'

Tom's eyes flicked towards Ava for a moment.

'Okay, Mum. No, I understand . . . I promise. Okay, Mum, love you. Be careful and ring when there's more news.'

Tom stood still, shoulders hunched, facing the wall.

# HONESTY

'Tom, are the sheep okay?' asked Ava. 'Have they found Hope?'

Tom sighed and turned to face her.

'The sheep rustlers had scarpered by the time Mum and Dad got there, but they've managed to make the field secure again. They think about half the flock have been taken.'

'Oh no!' cried Ava.

'Dad reckons they would've got more if you

hadn't surprised them. The police are searching for them, and so are Mum and Dad. We know all the vehicles and trailers around here, so they'll spot anything suspicious.'

Ava looked out of the window. It was still dark, so she wasn't sure how much luck they'd have finding the trailer. She swallowed and looked at Tom.

'And Hope?' she whispered.

Tom's face crumpled as he sat down opposite her.

'I'm sorry, Ava. There's no sign of her yet.'

Ava bit her lip, trying to push away the overwhelming feeling of despair that flooded through her. She had to stay strong, to think about the best way to find Hope.

'They'll find her, Ava – I know they will.'

Ava's eyes blazed at Tom.

'She wouldn't be missing if you'd trusted me.'

Tom hung his head.

'Why do you hate me so much, Tom?' asked Ava, her voice quiet now.

Tom looked up sharply, his eyes wide in surprise.

'I don't hate you!'

'Well, it sure feels like you do sometimes,' Ava replied. 'All you do is make me feel stupid. You never want to spend any time with me. You're even embarrassed of me in front of your friends!'

Tom took a deep breath and sighed.

'I don't hate you, Ava,' he said quietly. 'Far from it. I didn't want you to hang out with my friends because . . . Well, because I didn't want them to like you more than me.'

Ava blinked in surprise.

'What?'

Tom looked away. 'You've always been so much cooler than me, Ava. You're good at everything too.'

'No, I'm not!' said Ava.

'The stuff you do back at home, the sports, the

classes – all I ever hear about is what new thing you're doing that I don't do. All I'm good at is farming. Whenever you came to the farm before, you weren't interested in it. I thought you were stuck up and didn't want to get your hands dirty, but that kinda suited me. The one thing I was good at that you weren't.'

'I never knew you felt like that.'

Tom sniffed. 'You never really spoke to me, so how would you know? When you started showing an interest in the farm this time, I . . . I *wanted* you to be bad at it. But you weren't and that was annoying. I'm sorry, Ava. I guess I just *wanted* you to be wrong about the things you saw. You're right – none of this would have happened if I'd listened. I didn't want to bother Mum and Dad either, but I should have told them. No matter how busy they were.'

Tom held his head in his hands, and Ava couldn't

tell if he was crying. Ava's head was swirling with it all. The kidnapped sheep, Hope missing and now this. As she looked at Tom, her anger softened. If Tom was being honest, then so should she.

'The truth is, Tom, I'm not that great at any of the stuff I do at home – I'm only trying to find what I *am* good at. The sad thing is that I'm only ever *okay* at it all. I'd love to be as good at something as you are – you're amazing on the farm. I'm sorry I never took any interest before. I honestly didn't think I'd like it, but I do.'

Tom looked up at her, his eyes red.

'But you're good with animals, Ava. Look how well you've done with Hope.'

'But I totally messed up with the chickens.'

Tom nodded and gave her a weak smile.

'But maybe if I'd been a better cousin, I would've shown you how to do stuff properly. Truth is, Ava, I feel just as guilty about the fox as you.'

Tom's bottom lip trembled. Ava's heart ached for the mess they'd got themselves in.

'I'll be back home soon and I'll really miss it here. You're lucky, you know. From what I've seen, you've got a great bunch of friends. I don't really have any at home and I guess I was a little envious of that. *And* you've got Whistledown.' Ava paused. 'It's funny, my parents have always encouraged me to find that "thing" I love – like they love their work. And like you all love the farm. Turns out, maybe farming *is* for me too. I can't wait to get out of bed and see the animals, and I never thought that sleeping on the floor of a cold barn would be something I'd get excited about!'

Tom looked at her across the table and smiled.

'You do love it, don't you?'

Ava nodded.

'The farm is your thing, Tom. That will never change. But I'd love to share it with you when I'm here. There were a few times this week where I think we even had fun!' Ava laughed softly and her cousin smiled.

'I did actually enjoy your company on a couple of occasions,' Tom said with a wink.

'Maybe we're stronger together?' suggested Ava.

'Maybe,' said Tom. 'I promise to listen to you in the future, Ava.'

The shrill ring of the house phone made them jump again. Tom answered and a smile spread across his face.

'Okay,' he said into the phone. 'Fingers crossed. See you soon!'

He slammed down the handset and turned to Ava.

'The police think they've found the trailer a few miles away. Mum and Dad are headed there now to check it out. They think the sheep might still be in it!'

'So, Hope might be there too?' said Ava. Her heart was pounding.

'I'm sure she will, Ava. Where else could she be?'

# Chapter Twenty-seven

# THE WHISTLEDOWN FLOCK

Just over an hour, two cups of tea and a large slice of cake later, Ava and Tom heard the truck pull up. The door opened and a weary-looking Uncle John and Aunt Kitty stepped into the kitchen.

'Any more news?' asked Tom, hopping from foot to foot.

Aunt Kitty clicked on the kettle.

'We've got them back,' she said with a tired smile.

Tears of relief welled in Ava's eyes.

'What happened?' she asked.

Uncle John sat down, throwing his cap onto the table.

'The police spotted a trailer abandoned a few villages away. We headed over and sure enough, there it was.'

'And all the sheep were still inside?' asked Ava.

'Amazingly, they were,' said Aunt Kitty.

'Police reckon the thieves got spooked,' said Uncle John.

'Ava told them she'd called the police,' said Tom, looking proudly at her. 'Maybe that was enough to make them think twice?'

Aunt Kitty set mugs of tea on the table, kissing Ava lightly on her head as she did so.

'I think you're right.'

Aunt Kitty's face fell as she noticed Ava's ankle resting on the chair.

'What happened?'

'Oh, it's nothing,' said Ava, waving her aunt away. 'It feels much better after Tom helped me with it.'

Aunt Kitty looked at them both, her eyebrows raised in surprise.

'You two seem . . . different?' she said.

Ava and Tom smiled at each other.

'I think we've sorted things out,' said Ava.

Aunt Kitty's lips twitched into a smile as she checked on Ava's swollen ankle.

'Did the police catch them?' asked Tom.

'Nope,' said Uncle John. 'Apparently, there's been a spate of sheep rustling in the next county, so it seems they tried their luck over here as well. Trailer was stolen too.'

'They didn't account for our Ava though, did they?' said Aunt Kitty with a wink.

Ava lowered her bruised ankle to the floor and put some weight on it. It didn't feel great, but thankfully it wasn't any worse.

'And where do you think you're going?' asked Aunt Kitty, sipping her tea.

'I'm going to check on Hope,' said Ava, limping towards the door. 'Is she back in the barn?'

Uncle John and Aunt Kitty exchanged a look. Aunt Kitty set down her mug of tea and reached for Ava's hand.

'She wasn't in the trailer, sweetheart.'

'What? What do you mean?' Ava felt panic rising inside her.

Uncle John cleared his throat.

'When we brought the trailer back and let the sheep out, we didn't see Hope amongst them.'

A wave of nausea washed over Ava.

'But . . . but where is she?'

Aunt Kitty stood and put her arms round Ava.

'It's really dark, sweetheart. We couldn't see her, but it doesn't mean she's not there.'

'I need to find her!'

Ava hobbled towards the front door, but Aunt Kitty caught her arm.

'There's no point going out now. We need to wait for daylight. When we've had some sleep and a bit of breakfast, we can all look for her properly.'

Panic and exhaustion made Ava's brain fuzzy. Half of her agreed with Aunt Kitty, and the other half wanted to race down to the field. She knew it was pointless searching in the dark though.

'Come on, sweetheart. Let's get you upstairs. You must be shattered,' said Aunt Kitty softly.

'But I won't be able to sleep,' protested Ava.

'Your aunt's right,' said Uncle John. 'There's not much we can do now. We'll search in the morning when we're all fresh.'

Ava bit her lip. The last thing she wanted was to leave Hope out there on her own, but it seemed she had no choice.

Ava lay in bed, ankle throbbing. She hadn't closed her curtains so she could fix her eyes on the window, willing the sun to rise. Magpie the farm cat had found her way into Ava's room and had curled up at the bottom of her bed. Just having its quiet company made Ava feel better – she hadn't wanted to be alone. Slowly, the sky turned from grey to a red haze – it was definitely getting lighter.

Ava heard a gentle tap on her door. It was so quiet, she wondered at first if it was just the old farmhouse pipes. The tap sounded again.

'Hello?' whispered Ava.

The door opened a fraction and Tom's head popped round.

'Thought you might be awake,' he whispered, stepping into Ava's room, closing the door behind him. He was fully dressed and carrying a small rucksack.

'Ready?' he said, hovering by the door.

'Ready for what?' said Ava.

'Finding Hope.'

# Chapter Twenty-eight

# HOPE

Tom and Ava crept silently down the stairs. Tom motioned to Ava to avoid certain creaky steps so they didn't wake anyone. They made it to the front door, grabbing their coats on the way. Tom helped Ava into her wellies, which wasn't easy with her swollen ankle.

'Wait here,' whispered Tom, handing her his rucksack.

Ava stepped out into the crisp early morning air

and shivered. Without the sun fully risen, it was cold, and Ava had everything crossed that Hope was warm enough, wherever she was. Tom reappeared with his bike.

'Hop on then,' he whispered.

'There's only one seat,' said Ava with a frown.

Tom tried to stifle a laugh.

'Course there is. You get on the seat, and I'll pedal in front.'

Ava hesitated.

'Have you never piggybacked on a bike before?' asked Tom.

Ava shook her head.

'You've still got a lot to learn, Ava! It'll be better than you limping down the track.'

Ava swung her leg over and balanced on the seat. Tom set off, leaning forward to give her as much room as possible behind him. The cold early morning wind stung Ava's cheeks as they sped down the farm track. The bike wobbled on a loose stone and Ava hung on tightly to her cousin.

The bike screeched to a halt as they arrived at the gate to the bottom fields. Tom helped Ava off and opened the gate for her. He took the rucksack and pulled out a couple of torches.

'It's light enough to see now, but we can use these to check any dark hiding places she could have wriggled into,' he said, handing her one.

'Thanks, Tom,' said Ava with a worried smile.

As Ava took in the expanse of field, she was relieved to see it was full of mothers and lambs, all safe and sound. But she needed to find *her* lamb. They began to scour the field, calling out to Hope. It was slow-going, their search hampered by Ava's ankle and Tom's unwillingness to leave her on her own.

There was no sign of Hope in the field, so they began to search the thick, dark hedgerows along the edges. Ava silently thanked Tom for the torches; it was a good idea to bring them.

They made it round the field and up to the gate that bordered the road. A brand-new lock and chain was secured round it. Ava stopped to catch her breath. Her ankle burned with pain, and worry squeezed her chest. The woodland fence lay before them – the last place left to check. Ava felt Tom's hand on her shoulder.

'We'll find her, Ava.'

Ava hobbled to the fence and examined the overgrown bushes that were peppered along it.

With each painful step, and no sign of Hope, Ava's panic grew. She came to the bush she'd hidden behind on her stakeout. Visions of the night's events played in her head. Hot, desperate tears prickled in her eyes.

'Wait a minute,' said Tom, bending down to look at the fence by the bush. 'This bit's broken. It looks like something could have pushed through.'

A glimmer of hope rippled inside Ava.

Tom climbed over the fence and held out his hand to help Ava over, but she hesitated. The weak rays of sunlight hadn't reached into the woodland yet, making it look dark and foreboding.

'Come on, Ava,' encouraged Tom.

'I've not had the best experiences in the woods,' said Ava nervously.

'The woods are one of my favourite places on the whole farm!' said Tom with a grin. 'I know them like the back of my hand. You'll be fine with me.

I'm sure you'll love them too one day.'

Tom's enthusiasm gave Ava the extra courage she needed. With Tom's help, she made it over the fence and into the woodland.

'You look left – I'll look right,' Tom instructed. 'Use your torch if you need to.'

'Hope!' called Ava. 'Hope, where are you?'

Ava's calls were met with deafening silence as they continued deeper into the woods.

Tom stopped suddenly.

'Shh,' he said, listening intently. 'Call her again.'

'Hope! Hope . . .'

They heard a faint sound.

'This way,' said Tom.

They carefully picked their way through the tree roots and undergrowth.

'Hope?' called Ava.

The sound was clearer this time, but very weak. Ava exchanged a worried glance with Tom.

'We need to hurry, Tom. Hope could be in trouble.'

They shone their torches onto the woodland floor, searching for any sign of Hope amongst the fallen branches and tufts of grass. The sun had risen higher, but instead of helping them to see more clearly, it created dark pockets and shadows that all looked Hope-shaped to Ava.

'Hope!' called Ava again.

*Baa.*

This time, it was crystal clear. Weak but one hundred per cent Hope.

Tom pointed. 'It came from over there!'

They hurried in the direction of Hope's cry. The woodland floor dipped in front of them into a deep ditch. Tom held out an arm to stop Ava sliding down into it.

'The old ruins,' explained Tom, his breathing fast and excited. 'Dad says it's some sort of old settlement. They run right through the woodland. Some bits are deeper than others.'

'So, Hope could have fallen in?' asked Ava.

*Baa.*

Tom and Ava looked along the ditch in the direction of the sound.

'There she is!' shouted Ava.

Hope was lying in the bottom, a few metres along from where they stood. She tried to stand but fell back to the ground with a thump.

'I'll get her,' said Tom. 'There's no way you'll climb down there with that ankle.'

Every bone in Ava's body wanted to get to Hope, but Tom was right – she'd never make it down, let alone back up again. She watched helplessly as Tom skidded down the steep bank. He reached the bottom and ran towards Hope. The lamb seemed startled, but didn't struggle when Tom gently picked her up. He raced back and tried to climb out of the ditch. His feet slipped on the steep, leaf-covered sides and he slid all the way back.

Ava scrambled painfully towards a tree growing partway down the side of the ditch. Gingerly, she made her way towards it, blocking out the agony in her ankle. Grasping the knobbly trunk with one hand, she leaned forward, reaching out towards Tom.

Tom ran up the side of the ditch again, throwing out an arm to Ava, the other arm holding on to Hope. Their hands met, gripping each other tightly. Ava gritted her teeth as she pulled Tom towards her until he could grab onto the tree. Tom hauled himself up to safety before helping Ava back up to the top too.

'Hope!' breathed Ava.

Tom handed her the lamb and Ava gasped.

'She's really cold.'

Tom nodded, lines of worry etched on his face.

'We need to get her back to the farmhouse, Ava. I think she may have broken her leg.'

Ava looked at Hope and winced. One of her front legs was bent at an unnatural angle.

They made their way out of the woods as quickly as they could. But just as they reached the fence-line, Ava saw someone standing in the field.

'Tom!' she whispered. 'Someone's there.'

'I'll take a look,' said Tom, an uneasy expression etched on his face.

Using the bushes for cover and crouching low to the floor, he made his way unseen towards the field. Suddenly he stood up and turned to face Ava.

'It's Mum!' he shouted with a grin.

Relief swept through Ava as she limped towards the field, Hope clasped tightly in her arms. Sure enough, as she got closer, she could make out Aunt Kitty. Uncle John was there too, relief on their faces as they caught sight of Tom and Ava.

'We found her!' said Tom, waving to his mum and dad.

Aunt Kitty took Hope as Uncle John helped Ava over the fence.

'She doesn't look too good, Ava,' said Aunt Kitty. 'You'll have to work your magic on her again.'

'I *promise* I will,' said Ava with a smile.

# Chapter Twenty-nine

# NEW BEGINNINGS

Hope lay in a box in front of the oven, reminding Ava of her first few days at Whistledown Farm. She'd warmed up since they'd brought her back, but it didn't stop Ava anxiously chewing her thumbnail instead of eating the scrambled eggs Aunt Kitty had made her. A knock on the door made Ava jump.

'Hello, hello. Only me!'

A tall grey-haired woman stepped into the kitchen. She was wearing blue waterproof trousers and a sweatshirt with a white emblem.

'Cassie, thanks for coming so quickly,' said Aunt Kitty, giving the woman a brief hug.

Ava read the emblem on her sweatshirt.

*Perrywick Veterinary Practice.*

Ava's face lit up. 'You're the vet!'

'And you must be Ava! The young lady who has a knack for saving lambs,' said Cassie, her bright eyes twinkling. 'Where's the patient?'

'Hope's here,' said Ava, pointing towards the box.

'Hope . . .' repeated Cassie, flashing Aunt Kitty a smile. 'Well, let's have a look at *Hope*, shall we?'

Cassie examined Hope, listening to her chest, checking her temperature and finally inspecting her front leg.

'It's definitely broken, but we can sort it,' she said warmly.

Cassie reached down to pick up Hope.

'Happy to give me a hand, Ava?' she asked.

'Can I?' replied Ava excitedly.

'Course. Hang on to her while I get everything ready.'

Cassie laid Hope on Ava's lap while she rummaged in her bag.

'First things first. I need to put her broken leg in a cast. She's not going to like it, so if you can hold on to her, I can make sure the bone is straight.'

Cassie worked quickly and efficiently. Hope hardly flinched as Cassie wrapped her leg with a roll of something she'd dipped in water.

'This will set hard and allow the bone to heal. We might have to change it as Hope grows, but she'll be right as rain in a few weeks.'

'Thank you,' said Ava, giving Cassie one of her best smiles.

'Do you want to finish it?' asked Cassie, holding out the last bit of wrap.

'Yes, I'd like that a lot!' said Ava.

Cassie lifted Hope and put her onto her own lap, with the grace and efficiency of years' handling animals. Ava began to wrap the rest of Hope's leg, her hands shaking ever so slightly.

'Perfect!' said Cassie. 'You should pop down to the surgery and help out. I could always use a good pair of hands like yours. When she's warmed up and the cast has set, she'll be fine to go back to the barn. Keep doing what you're doing, Ava. She's in great condition!'

Ava beamed as she watched Cassie pack up her things and leave. She looked at Hope sleeping soundly on her lap. She felt her chest tighten at the thought of having to leave her.

Later that day, Tom and Ava took Hope back to the barn. They laid fresh straw, making sure she was comfortable. Ava set up her sleeping bag and pillow, ready to sleep next to Hope again. Aunt Kitty had even made a 'midnight feast' so it would be extra special.

'I'll be back in a minute,' said Tom, disappearing from the barn.

Ava tickled under Hope's chin. She was going to miss her, but knew she'd be well looked after. Besides, as soon as her leg healed, she'd be able to go out in the field with the rest of the growing lambs. Ava knew Hope would love having sheep friends.

Tom reappeared, carrying a large bundle.

'What's all that?' asked Ava.

'Thought I'd sleep over with you and Hope tonight,' he said, unfurling a sleeping bag.

Ava grinned.

'We'd like that, wouldn't we, Hope?'

*Baa.*

Tom and Ava laughed.

The barn door opened and Uncle John peered round.

'You two might want to get yourselves to the chicken barn,' he said with a smile.

Tom gave Ava a piggyback to the barn to save her hobbling on her twisted ankle. They skidded to a halt in front of the incubator.

'Shh,' whispered Tom. 'We need to stay quiet so we don't put them off.'

'Is that actually a thing?' said Ava.

'Course,' said Tom.

They peered at the eggs, and Ava almost squealed in delight. One egg had a crack going nearly halfway round its shell.

'Keep watching,' whispered Tom. 'You'll see the chick tapping the egg.'

Ava fixed her eyes on the crack line. Moments later, she saw something move inside. The crack bulged wider and then shrank back together again.

'I saw a beak, Tom! Is it pecking its way out?'

Tom shook his head.

'There's a little bump on top of its beak. The chicks tap all the way round in a circle, breaking the shell with the bump until they can push the shell apart.'

'Looks like this one's nearly there!' said Ava excitedly.

'Not long now,' said Tom. 'It can sometimes take a whole day for it to get out though.'

Suddenly the egg broke apart. A tiny, wet

prehistoric-looking creature rolled out and began chirping.

'Ugh, they look weird!' said Ava.

'So would you if you'd spent three weeks squashed inside an egg!'

Ava laughed.

'Don't worry, it'll dry off in a few hours and look really cute,' said Tom.

'Look!' said Ava, pointing to another egg. 'That one's rocking!'

'That'll be next then,' said Tom with a nod.

'I'm going to miss all this,' said Ava quietly.

Tom nudged her gently.

'We're going to miss you too, Ava.'

# Chapter Thirty

# HOME

The day Ava had been looking forward to when she'd first arrived at Whistledown Farm, but had recently begun to dread, had finally arrived. Her mum and dad were on their way from the airport – they'd be there in a couple of hours. Ava was in Tom's favourite spot, sitting on the bales in the hay barn, trying to get excited about going home. She'd missed her parents a lot and couldn't wait to see them, but she was going to miss everything about

Whistledown Farm. Ava looked out at the expanse of green fields around her. Her view would be very different back home.

She and Tom had spent the last few days almost permanently in each other's company. He'd shown her so much, saying he was going to cram everything they could into the rest of the holiday.

They'd explored the woods, seen the last of the lambs being born, watched the eggs hatch in the incubator and helped Hope get stronger. Ava's emotions felt complicated as she thought of Hope. She was happy Hope was up and about, hobbling around on her cast, but Ava was going to miss her very much. She would have to ask her mum and dad to bring her back to Whistledown more often.

She slid down from Tom's hiding place, wincing at the pain shooting through her ankle. Like Hope's injury, it was getting better, but she would be taking it home as a memento.

Ava decided to take one last walk round the farm. She watched the sheep with their lambs, listened to the birds in the hedgerows and counted the daffodils, trying to commit everything to memory. She took a shortcut back to the farmhouse, crossing Harris's field. He wandered across to nuzzle her hands and her pockets.

'Here you go, boy,' she whispered, pulling out a carrot.

She looked up at the house as Harris munched on his treat. Her parents were already here!

'Time to go, Harris. I'll be back soon though, I promise.' She felt a pang of sadness as she ran her fingers through his mane one last time.

Ava headed towards the house, the excitement building at the thought of seeing her parents. She was surprised to see Tom sitting on the doorstep, stroking Magpie on his lap.

'What are you doing out here? Have you been put on the naughty step?'

Ava laughed, but Tom looked worried.

'I'm not sure what's going on. Your mum and dad arrived, and the next minute I was chucked out.'

A tingle of unease crept across the back of Ava's neck.

Tom gave her a friendly nudge. 'Maybe my mum and dad are telling yours what a nightmare we've been,' he said with a wry smile.

'I hope not!' she said, slipping past Tom.

'Ava, wait – we're not allowed in!'

She burst through the kitchen door and four faces turned to look at her.

'Mum! Dad!'

Ava flew towards her parents and flung her arms round them.

'I missed you so much!'

Ava buried her head into them. She couldn't

believe they were actually here! A wave of happiness washed over her.

'We missed you, too,' said her mum, prising herself away from Ava to get a good look at her. She kissed Ava on her forehead before pulling her in for another hug.

'I think you've got taller!' said her dad, ruffling Ava's dark hair. 'Must be all that country air and Aunt Kitty's dinners!'

Ava felt herself blush.

'Well, tell us all about it,' said Ava's mum, cradling Ava's face in her hands. 'How much trouble have you been causing?'

Her mum and dad laughed, but Ava felt her face pale.

'It's all fine – everything's fine. Tom and I are good friends now. Aren't we, Tom?'

Tom nodded vigorously.

'Well . . . that's good,' said her mum, with an

expression of mild confusion. She turned to look at Aunt Kitty, who was busying herself making a pot of tea.

Ava leaned forward and hugged her mum again. She breathed in the familiar scent of shampoo and perfume. She stayed there for a moment, taking it all in.

'I missed you, Mum,' muttered Ava, as she reluctantly pulled away. 'Don't ever go away again!'

Her mum's face fell.

An awkward silence descended on the kitchen, and Ava looked from one adult to another.

'What's going on?' asked Ava. 'And why was Tom outside on the step? Did something happen in Chicago?'

Something was definitely wrong.

'Everything's fine, Ava,' said her mum, indicating for her to sit at the table. 'Chicago was great – wasn't it, Dave?'

Ava's dad nodded. 'Great. Chicago was great.' He seemed nervous.

Ava frowned. Her parents were acting weird.

'And how was the trial? Did the antibiotics work?' asked Ava. Her mind was racing.

'Yes . . . that was great too,' replied her mum, an odd smile fixed on her face.

'Oh, for heaven's sake, you two, just talk to her about it!' said Aunt Kitty, setting the teapot down with a thump.

Ava stared at her parents, waiting for whatever was coming. What weren't they telling her?

'Well, that's just it. Chicago was great. The trial was great,' said Ava's mum.

'*We* were great,' cut in her dad.

Ava's parents laughed nervously. Her mum cleared her throat.

'It all went well. So well, in fact, that they've offered to extend our contract.'

Ava held her breath.

'They'd like us to go back to Chicago to finish what we started. We're on the verge of a brilliant breakthrough!'

Her dad leaned forward.

'We just need a little longer to get everything finished. It would only be for about three months, tops. There's a great school round the corner from the laboratory. I'm sure you'd love it, Ava.'

Ava's mouth went dry as her mum took hold of her hands.

'Your dad and I have talked about it non-stop all the way home. We think it will be great for all of us. You'll make new friends, see a new country . . .'

Ava blinked, slowly understanding what her parents were saying.

'But I don't want to move to Chicago,' said Ava quietly.

'It wouldn't be for ever,' her mum said, smoothing

Ava's hair. 'It'll be an adventure, just like these last couple of weeks.'

Tears pricked at Ava's eyes.

'I don't want to go,' she whispered.

Ava knew how busy her mum and dad were at home and the long hours they often worked. It would be the same in Chicago. What would she do while they were working? She'd be lonely again.

Aunt Kitty coughed and everyone looked at her.

'Well, before you burst in, your mum and dad were telling me about this amazing job offer.'

The look she gave Ava told her she should try and be a little happier for them.

'I was also about to suggest an *alternative* option.'

'An alternative?' asked Ava's dad.

'Yes,' said Aunt Kitty. 'How would you *all* feel about Ava staying with us? As you said, it is just for a few months.'

The room fell silent. Ava felt Tom nudge her from behind.

'Well . . .' said Ava's mum, turning to look at her husband. 'I guess it's something we *could* consider.'

Something unspoken passed between Ava's parents.

'It would be up to Ava though,' said her dad softly.

'Your dad and I would really like to see our work through to the end – it's a great opportunity. The new antibiotics could save a lot of lives. We're sure you'd love it over there for a few months. But we don't want to drag you halfway round the world if you're going to be unhappy.'

'This is really important to you, isn't it?' said Ava.

'It is, love. But you're *more* important to us. So, you can choose what you want to do. You can come with us to Chicago, or you can take up your aunt's very kind offer *if* you promise to call us every day.'

'And we'd come back and see you, every chance

we got,' added Ava's dad, leaning forward and looking serious.

'Or . . . we'll turn the offer down and stay at home,' said her mum, her eyes searching Ava's.

Ava smiled at her parents. It felt great to have them back. But she was torn. Her heart ached at the thought of them going away again — but the idea of them not finishing their work because of her felt worse. She'd enjoyed her stay at Whistledown Farm more than she'd imagined she would, even with everything that had happened. She knew she would miss the farm terribly — the animals, her aunt and uncle, Tom and especially Hope. None of the options were perfect — life rarely was — but she knew in her gut what she wanted to do.

'You don't need to decide right now. We wouldn't need to go back until the end of the summer. There's plenty of time to think about it,' said her mum softly.

'I don't need time to think about it,' said Ava. 'I'd love to stay at Whistledown Farm!'

Ava's mum and dad pulled her into a tight hug again. Ava held on to them, not wanting it to end.

'We love you, Ava,' whispered her parents together.

Everyone took their cups of tea and a plate of freshly baked ginger biscuits outside to sit on the patio that overlooked the fields. Ava disappeared for a moment before coming back with Hope in her arms. She set the lamb down and introduced Hope to her mum and dad.

*Baa.*

Ava looked out across the green rolling hills of the valley and then back at Hope, who was happily accepting a chin tickle from her mum. Her aunt and uncle were talking about the weather with her dad, and Tom was making short work of the biscuits. Ava smiled. She felt happier than she had in a long time, and she knew she'd made the right decision to stay at Whistledown Farm.

In fact, she was really looking forward to it.

A WHISTLEDOWN FARM ADVENTURE

# Book 2!

Coming
October 2024